LADYBUCK ON LADYBUCK

Seven Lesbian Tales Of The Tingleverse

CHUCK TINGLE

No matter who you are or what your preferred pound, there's always room for you in The Tingleverse.

- Chuck Tingle

CONTENTS

SENTIENT LESBIAN JET SKI GETS ME OFF

As a city dweller, there's nothing quite like a girl's weekend away to reset my mind and bring me back in touch with the things that matter most. During my Monday to Friday grind, there's very little time for introspection, and although my co-workers are very sweet in their own way, I'd hardly consider us friends. You really don't realize just how soul crushing it is until, eventually, the weekend arrives and you look back in wonder at how you actually managed to make it this far.

Now, I'm trying my best to focus on the world in front of me, gazing out the windows as we cruise deeper and deeper into these desert canyons, twisting along a desolate highway towards the lake.

I've never been out here before, but my friends all say it's an absolutely magical experience. I'm inclined to believe them, but right now there's not much to look at on our journey. No matter where I set my gaze I see nothing but endless, rolling hills of yellow, the grass dried and dead and strangely surreal under the brilliant blue sky.

I wonder what Gorba would've thought about all this.

"You thinking about Gorba?" my friend, Rachel questions, glancing over at me from the driver's seat with a slight smirk on her face.

"How the fuck do you do that?" I question. "Are you reading my mind?"

Rachel shrugs. "I just know you. We've been friends for almost a decade now."

I let out a long sigh, continuing to stare out through the window before me as the scenery passes us by. I suppose that's the one good thing about the daily worker's grind, you don't have much time to think about your recent breakup.

"I'm sorry, I'm trying not to let it get me down," I continue. "Breakups are hard, though."

Rachel nods. "Yeah, but it's been like six months. It's time to get out there and start seeing what the world has to offer. You've been wallowing a lot."

"I've been coming out with you!" I protest. "We get chocolate milks every weekend!"

"And you *wallow* the whole time," Rachel continues. "Gorba was a nice girl, but *you* are amazing, and you deserve to be with a woman who understands that."

I know she's right, but brains are a complicated thing to navigate. Just because I'm aware I need to get over Gorba, doesn't mean this emotional clarity will come on any faster. However, a weekend on the water with my girls while the sun beams down on my skin sounds like a great start, even if it's six months too late.

Suddenly, the car comes up over a crest in the road, revealing a startlingly glorious vista. A slight gasp escapes my throat when I see it, taken off guard by just how blue this enormous turquoise lake really is. For as desolate as our drive had been, this dazzling source of water brings about all kinds of fresh greenery, the edge of the lake lined with tall trees and what appears to be handful of restaurants and hotels.

"Oh my fucking god," one of my friends offers from the backseat.

I'm excited, but I can help shaking a strange, creeping dread that bubbles up within me. It's like the happier I get, the more worried and anxious I am that it will all come crashing down when I start thinking about Gorba.

Where would Gorba want to stay if we were here together? What if I'm out of cell phone range when Gorba calls and tries to meet back up?

I catch Rachel glancing over at me again, clearly aware of the mixed emotions I'm going through right now. My friend says nothing, but I'm glad to know she's here by my side.

Lower and lower into the valley our car winds, eventually finding ourselves right on the edge of the beautiful turquoise lake. This place would normally be packed with tourists, but we're getting a little late in the vacation season, giving us a bit of room to breathe as we enjoy or surroundings.

Soon enough, we're pulling up to the front of our luxurious lakeside hotel. I climb out of the car and gaze up at the building before me, taking a deep, full breath of the fresh air around us.

"First we check in, then we pound some chocolate milk, then we hit the lake," Rachel cries out. "I heard they have jet skis."

The very mention of these aquatic vehicles causes my breath to catch in my throat. Gorba loved to jet ski and would talk about it all the time, a hobby that I personally never had much interest in. My ex would always take off to lakes in the area for days at a time.

"Maybe I'll just skip the water," I offer.

Rachel stops, turning her attention back to me while the rest of our crew heads insides and starts bringing bags up to the room. "Polly, you're not seriously going to stay inside this whole weekend are you?"

I shake my head. "No… it's just…"

"Gorba liked to jet ski," Rachel interjects.

I nod. "I'll lay out on the sand and watch you!" I suggest.

My friend lets out a long sigh, clearly disappointed, but finally accepts the simple fact this is where I'm at. "Fair enough," Rachel finally replies.

I'm laying out on the beach in my yellow bikini, watching as the rest of the gang walks up and down the nearby dock and takes their pick from an assortment of colorful jet skis. I've got a blanket under me, a cool chocolate milk in one hand and a good book in the other, so I'm not exactly having a terrible time. Still, it's hard to watch everyone else laughing excitedly from my place on the sidelines. For a moment I actually consider strolling over to join them, but the second these thoughts enter my mind, I also find myself overwhelmed with visions of my ex-girlfriend, imagining what it would be like to ride the waves alongside her.

Instead of springing into action, I lay back against the fabric below me, feeling the heat radiate up through this blanket and into my back. I open up my book and begin to read, excited to see what comes next. It's a beautiful romance novel from one of my favorite authors, Dr. Chuck Tingle, and although he only writes about encounters between two men, I find it to be quite an enjoyable read. I'm only interested in women myself, but I can appreciate a well-crafted story, especially when the message is as uplifting as

Chuck's.

I just wish he'd write a story about two women falling in love for once. It's not something he's ever done before, and as far as I know he has no plans to, but it just might be enough to get my mind off of Gorba. If there's one thing Gorba didn't like, it's Chuck Tingle.

I've just about settled into the story before me when, suddenly, my focus is broken by the loud roar of three jet skis taking off from the dock, my friends hooting and hollering as they fly out across the lake with their fists in the air. I watch them go, smiling wide.

When I turn back to the book, I suddenly find myself having a little trouble picking up where I left off. I could've sworn the last sentence I'd read was at the top of the page, but none of these words make any sense, referencing things that I'm not even sure were in this erotic tale just seconds earlier.

"Maybe today's your lucky day," I read aloud. "Maybe I *will* write a tingler just for you."

I'm not exactly sure who these words are directed at, as they only appear in quotes after I've read them out loud. Until that exact moment, they're just ink on the page.

"Are you talking to me?" I question, receiving no response until I glance a little farther in the book.

Yes, I'm talking to you, Polly, the text replies, addressing me directly.

I narrow my eyes, watching as the next paragraph describes me narrowing my eyes.

"What's going on?" I question aloud.

I'm writing to let you know that I'm sorry it took me so long to tell this dang story, the book informs me. *It's not that I didn't want to write a story for ladybucks who like ladybucks. That's a great preferred pound, buddy! It's just that I wanted to make sure I did it correctly. Now I have Chloe here editing and making sure everything is handled in a good way that proves love, because she likes ladybucks, too. She even picked out the dang cover models!*

"Okay," is all that I can think to say, the word falling limply from my mouth.

I know this is a lot to take in, buckaroo, talking to your author and all, the book continues. *So I'll let you be on your way. I just wanted to say that your unique way is so important, and that your preferred pound is something that proves love is real! I know you've had a hard time after your breakup, and that's okay, but now it's time to get out there and trot with your head held high. Have some fun! You're in a Tingler after all!*

I consider the author's words for a moment, still struggling to come to terms with the fact that I appear to be a character in a piece of erotic fiction. I'm trying to stay calm, but all of this is a lot to take in.

"So you're really... Chuck?" I question.

Yes, the next paragraph says flatly.

"Okay," is all that I can think to reply with.

I begin to close the book but notice something written at the bottom of the page that catches my attention.

You know, I've talked to a lot of characters, the words read, *but they're usually men, that's just the way the cookies crumb when you're talkin' bud on bud pounds. Gotta start visiting ladybuck timelines more, this is really nice.*

"Thanks Chuck," I offer in return, then close the book.

I lay back against my blanket, eyes closed as I think about how to process all this new information. If I'm just a character in a book, then maybe all this breakup drama isn't quite as important as it seemed. Based on what I know about Tinglers, we're probably nearing the halfway point, and so far I feel like I've spent a lot of time moping around.

Fictional or not, this life belongs to me, not Gorba.

I sit up abruptly, climbing to my feet and strolling over to the dock. I climb up onto the wooden platform and begin to stroll down its length, eventually arriving before a woman with a clipboard and a fanny pack.

"Jet ski rentals?" I question.

The woman nods.

"I'd like one," I continue.

"Twenty dollars for the hour," the woman replies, holding out her hand. "Pick whatever jet ski looks good to you. Keys are in the ignition."

I place a crisp twenty-dollar bill in the woman's hand and then begin to make my way along the rows and rows of aquatic vehicles, determining the best looking one for myself. Most of the jet skis are outrageously painted with brilliant neon designs that crisscross their bodies, a look that's certainly eye catching, but not exactly my style. I'm looking for something a little more thoughtful, a subtle external touch to a vehicle that wields plenty of power on the inside.

The farther along this dock I walk, the more my heart begins to sink, not quite finding what I'm looking for.

Finally, I arrive at the very last jet ski, and at this point I stop abruptly, my heart skipping a beat. The jet ski before me is absolutely gorgeous, perfectly curved in a way that sends an unexpected chill of arousal down my spine. Her paint job is understated and classy, not trying to prove anything with its simple pallet yet displaying a grand heaping of confidence.

"I'll take this one!" I call over to the woman next to me, who nods and waves me onward.

Carefully, I climb out onto the vehicle and straddle its well-crafted form, struggling to figure out what all of these strange nobs and buttons do. I would've expected to receive a bit more instruction, but I suppose I'll have to work with what I've got.

Once I've got a reasonably good idea of the basics, I turn the keys and watch as the jet ski comes roaring to life. Immediately, a mighty sense of adventure washes over me, carrying me away to a place where Gorba is nothing but a distant memory. I carefully back the vehicle out and then push it forward into drive, taking off like a rocket across the gloriously flat lake.

"Yeah!" I scream, calling out with excitement as my voice carries out over the water. "Yahoo!"

I'm pushing the limits of my comfort at this speed, but with nothing ahead of or behind me for miles, it feels safe enough.

It's not long before I finally manage to relax. The second this happens, however, another strange sensation begins to make its way across my body. Below me the seat is vibrating hard, not in a way that's painful, but with a speed that seems to perfectly match the wavelengths of my own body.

It feels incredible.

"Oh my god," I blurt, hunching forward a bit as I ride.

"Oh sorry about that!" I playful voice comes back to me from the front of the jet ski. "My motor is right under you, so if you go too fast it's gonna vibrate pretty hard."

I slow down immediately, causing the vibration against my clit to cease. "No, it's fine," I stammer. "I just… wasn't expecting that."

The jet ski shrugs. "Happens to a lot of people. It's okay."

"And you don't mind?" I question.

"Oh no!" the aquatic vehicle assures me. "It's all part of the job."

Something about the way she says this actually hurts me slightly. I understand what just happened was a simple matter of anatomy, but it's hard to not let that blissful erotic sensation blossom into something more.

"What's your name?" I finally question, trying to change the subject.

"Limon Crims," offers the beautiful jet ski, "and you?"

"I'm Polly," I offer.

"You out here by yourself?" Limon continues.

I glance around the lake, trying to spot my friends as they horse around somewhere out on the water. It seems I've driven Limon and me around the edge of a peninsula and into a small cove, so there's not much to look at.

"I'm here with my friends," I explain, "but I don't really know what happened to them."

"Should we go track them down?" the jet ski questions.

I consider her offer for a moment, realizing suddenly that I have a choice to make. Rachel and the girls will be fine on their own, and if there's one thing they'd want for me on this vacation, it's to follow along the threads of any romantic connections that I find along the way.

"Actually, I was thinking we could take a break on the beach over here," I suggest. "We can go find my friends in a minute but... you seem really cool and it'd be great to get to know you."

"Sure!" Limon replies.

We putter towards the beach until, eventually, I can feel the sand beginning to slow us down as it rubs across the sentient jet ski's belly. At this point I hop out, feeling the pleasant sensation of the cool water between my toes as I walk to the edge of dry land. Limon remains half submerged, watching me with her beautiful blue eyes.

This is the first time I've actually gotten a good look at the jet ski's face, and I'm utterly blown away by just how ravishing she is. Her look is playful and wild, with huge eyes that seem to always have a slight sparkle behind them. Her jet ski body is perfectly proportioned, with plentiful curves along her smoothly rounded edge.

"How long have you been on this lake?" I ask, trying my best to make conversation with the beautiful vehicle.

"Since this story began," the jet ski offers. "So not long."

I furrow my brow in confusion. "Wait... you know we're just characters in a book, too?" I question.

The jet ski nods. "I've always known. What about you?"

"I just found out when Chuck started writing to me through a book,"

I explain.

The gorgeous jet ski laughs. "A book within a book, huh? That's very meta."

I shrug. "Who knows, maybe this book is also being read by someone who *also* doesn't realize they're in a Tingler."

"A book, within a book, within a book," the jet ski continues.

Now the both of us are laughing, unable to keep a straight face any longer as we consider just how ridiculous that idea is. Despite my powerful attraction to the watercraft, I'm slowly starting to feel more and more at ease with her. It seems like I should be incredibly intimidated by her extreme beauty, yet for whatever reason, I'm not. In fact, all I want is to get even closer to her, to make her a central character in my life.

I realize suddenly just how long the two of us have been sitting here in silence, relaxing in this lush cove while the rest of the world continues to pass by around us. We stare deep into one another's eyes, saying more with a single expression than words ever could.

Slowly, Limon begins to scoot up the beach towards me, closer and closer until she's resting directly in front of my body. I sit up as well, the tension building between us until, finally, it breaks.

The next thing I know, I'm kissing this beautiful jet ski deeply on her mouth, the two of us giving into the carnal desires that have been bubbling up from within. My hands being to explore the glorious topography of her sculpted jet ski form, rubbing up and down the smooth front section.

Meanwhile, Limon starts doing the same to me, rubbing up and down my legs as she creeps closer and closer towards my pussy. I tremble and quake, the anticipation almost too much to bear until, finally, the tension breaks and my bikini bottoms are slipped away. I'm now completely exposed to the gorgeous jet ski.

"You want me to touch you?" Limon coos.

"Yes," I nod. "Please."

The jet ski smiles, teasing me a bit longer as causing the ache within my body to return once more, this time reaching an absolutely unbearable level.

"Maybe I will," Limon continues playfully.

"I need you," I beg.

Finally, the sentient jet ski has mercy, allowing a single finger to slip across my soaking wet pussy. I'd been yearning for her touch, but when it finally happens the sensation is startlingly potent, causing a short gasp of air to escape my lips. I push back into the sand, squirming slightly as Limon begins to rub my clit in slow, gentle circles.

At first I have a little trouble relaxing, but as the movement of the living vehicle continues, I begin to allow these waves of anxiety to wash away, replaced instead by a deep, aching pleasure. I rock my hips along with the beautiful jet ski's movements, my eyes shut tight as a soft whimper escapes my lips.

Suddenly, Limon stops, pulling her hand away. I'm instantly brought up and out from my deep state of relaxation, not quite sure what's happening, but moments later my fears are alleviated as I find that the jet ski has positioned herself directly before me, and she quickly gets to work licking my clit with her soft pink tongue.

"Oh my fucking god," I blurt. I reach my hand down and pull Limon even closer, helping to position her for the maximum amount of pleasure. "That feels so fucking good."

The two of us continue to rock together, falling into a solid rhythm as she licks me. Each pulsing movement sends a slight tingle of blissful sensation across my body, growing larger and larger until, eventually, I'm shaking hard with feelings of an impending climax. I have to admit, I'm not used to cumming this quickly, but it appears Limon knows exactly what she's doing.

"Don't stop. Just like that. Don't stop. Just like that," I start to repeat over and over again, the mantra falling out of my mouth in a soft groove that grows louder and louder with every passing round. Soon enough, I'm screaming out at the top of my lungs, my voice echoing across our tiny cove and bouncing back to us. "Don't fucking stop! Just like that!"

Suddenly, the building orgasm erupts within, causing me to throw my head back and let out a frantic scream. I completely lose myself in the moment, allowing my body to give into this carnal bliss and letting it take me over. I feel as though I'm floating outside my own physical form, hovering above the world and gazing down upon myself.

When the feeling finally passes I fall back against the sand, but instead of finding myself fucked silly and utterly spent, I'm even more energized than before. I want nothing more than to return the favor.

"Now it's my turn," I tell the jet ski, falling forward and crawling across the sand towards her.

It doesn't take long for me to realize, however, that Limon's pussy will be quite hard to get to, positioned directly on the underside of her body.

The sentient jet ski notices my dilemma, playfully smirking a bit as she eases back into the water.

"Don't worry," Limon coos. "As long as you don't mind taking a quick dip, you'll be fine."

It takes me a moment to understand what she's saying, but when it finally hits me I spring into action. By now the gorgeous living vehicle is floating out six or seven feet deep, leaving me plenty of room to run to the edge of the lake and dive in.

The cool water feels wonderful and relaxing against my skin, but I don't let it lull me into a state of contentment. I have work to do.

Gazing up from below, I spot Limon's beautiful jet ski pussy above me. I swim up to it, tilting my head back as I position myself. Seconds later, I'm lapping away at Limon's clit, dragging my tongue across her as she floats in circles above.

I can tell this beautiful jet ski is enjoying my technique, so gradually I push harder and harder against her with my tongue, eventually slipping two fingers within and creating a multitude of different sensations for her to enjoy.

I can her Limon starting to whimper and groan, the sound slightly muffled from my place down here under the water, but audible just the same. Louder and louder she grows, until finally she's screaming out with a powerful orgasm of her own, the internal muscles of her pussy clenching tight around my fingers while she cums.

Almost out of air, I quickly surface next to the sentient jet ski, taking in an enormous gasp or air.

"That was amazing," Limon gushes, red in the cheeks. "Let's get you one more time."

"Again?" I blurt, not even thinking of myself in this moment, but certainly appreciating my enthusiastic lover.

"Yep," Limon replies with a nod. "Get on!"

I do as I'm told, climbing out of the water and returning to my position on the living jet ski's back.

"This time... don't slow down," Limon instructs.

I smile and then hit the throttle, taking off back onto the lake once more. The wind is whipping hard against my face as the two of us fly forward across the pristine, glassy surface of the water. Below me, the seat begins to vibrate once again, immediately causing the first hints of yet another powerful orgasm to bubble up within me. Stronger they build, yet this time I don't pull away. Instead, I push the jet ski to go even faster.

"Oh fuck, oh fuck, oh fuck," I begin to murmer.

It's not long before the second orgasm hits me hard, sending powerful waves of erotic energy up and down my veins. It spills through me in a split second, and immediately I let up on the throttle of the jet ski as I shake in ecstasy.

When I finally finish, I find myself peacefully floating in the middle of the lake, utterly satisfied. Off in the distance, I can finally pick up the faintest sound of my friends hooting and hollering, having the time of their lives.

"We could go meet up with them if we hurry," the jet ski offers. "There's just not much time left on your rental."

Her words strike me deep, suddenly pulling me back down to reality. "Oh… yeah," I stammer.

There's an awkward silence between us. Limon is clearly thinking about something, choosing her words carefully.

"Unless… you want this to be a *thing*," the jet ski finally continues.

"A thing?" I question.

Limon nods. "If you'd want to be my girlfriend."

My eyes go wide, first with utter shock and then with heartwarming excitement. "Of course!" I blurt.

I wrap my arms tightly around the jet ski below me, holding her close.

"Do you think we did a good job?" I finally question.

"What do you mean?" Limon asks, a little confused.

"We're the first ladybuck on ladybuck Tingler, remember?" I continue. "I just hope we did it right."

"For who? This is about about me and you," Limon retorts. "We made love in our own way, that's what's important. Whether you're a character in a book, or a character reading a book who doesn't realize they're *also* in a book, your love is valid. That's not up to some omnipresent being to determine. Your love belongs to you."

"You're right," I reply, then find myself lingering on a single word. "You're saying we made *love?*"

"Made love," the jet ski repeats back to me with a smile. "Now lets go find your friends."

I hit the throttle and the two of us take off across the lake, excited for a weekend of fun and adventure. Right now, a recent breakup is the farthest thing from my mind.

MY T-REX BARBER IS A LESBIAN AND SHE EATS ME RIGHT

Few things are as stressful as an important job interview, especially when it's a job that you really, really want.

I've yearned to work in the biotech industry ever since I was a kid, watching educational videos on my own time while my friends were out playing in the yard and enjoying the sunshine. It's not to say I didn't do plenty of that myself, and physically exploring the world around you is an integral part of anyone's education, but I've also always had a drive to consume information as quickly and as thoroughly as possible.

Now I'm a strong, intelligent adult woman, and I'm ready to take the next big step in my professional life. After working in smaller laboratories for a good while and honing my chops, it's finally time for me to move onto one of the main biotech giants, or possibly even the biggest of them all.

I'm talking, of course, about Rubble Labs, the group that made headlines years ago when they were able to successfully clone a sentient butt. Ever since then, they've been continuing to push onward and upward in the world of biotech, advancing the scientific landscape leaps and bounds at a time.

Even Portork, the first living butt ever created, is now an international superstar.

It's a world that I desperately want to be a part of, and I've finally made it to the last interview in a series of many, the final hurtle before realizing my dream.

Suffice to say, tensions are high. I know I've got the mental chops for this elevated position, but the job I'm aiming for isn't just about lab work. It'd also be the face of the company during several meetings and mergers. I need to be cool, calm and collected at all times, and lately I certainly don't appear to be any of those things. I've been studying so hard that I've gradually let everything else slide, hardly getting enough sleep and letting my hair grow out way too long.

With only a day left to prepare, I suddenly realize there's just no more information that can fit within my mind. I'm all studied out, and right now what I need is a new pantsuit and a fresh haircut.

Unfortunately, today is Sunday, which means my usual hairstylist has shorter hours and they've already closed down for the evening. I could probably get something in extra early tomorrow morning, but honestly I'd rather be focused on the task at hand, which is knocking this meeting out of the park.

I'll just find a salon that's open and let them work their magic. How bad could it get, anyway?

I do a quick internet searches for salons nearby and discover there's a place just a few blocks from my apartment, close enough to walk. I immediately grab my purse and phone and head out the door, strolling onto the busy city sidewalk with confidence.

The din of the cars and people passing me by seems faint and muffled, this cacophonous sound pushed far from my mind by an overload of information that continues to swirl. I have answers for every question Rubble labs could possibly ask me, heaps of charts and graphs all memorized and at my disposal.

Relax, I tell myself. *Don't stress.*

It's only a ten-minute walk until I reach my destination, and when I arrive I'm thankful to find they have an immediate opening. I barely notice when the stylist introduces herself and asks what I wanna do with my hair, a question that makes me shrug apathetically.

"Just clean it up," I suggest, staring off into space as my mind continues to flood with information, going through my prepared interview answers over and over again in a seemingly endless loop.

The next thing I know the stylist is chopping away and my hair, swiveling me in her chair as she rotates my body from side to side, carefully crafting what I can only assume is a beautiful trim. I spend most of my time facing away from the massive mirror before my chair, but even if this weren't the case, I'd hardly notice what was happening. My thoughts are elsewhere.

Finally, my stylist steps back, taking in her handiwork with a satisfied nod.

"Yep, all done," the woman says proudly, snapping me back into reality.

My stylist swivels me around to face the mirror, which causes a startled gasp to escape my lips. At first I'm not quite sure what I'm seeing, as though this horrifying vision couldn't possibly belong to my own reality. I couldn't really be on the eve of the most important interview of my life with a haircut like this.

Whole patches of hair appear to be missing, an uneven set of layers crisscrossing my head without rhyme or reason. I'm usually pretty open to new and exciting fashion statements, but this goes well beyond anything like that.

"What the fuck," is all that I can think to say, the words tumbling out of my mouth as it continues to hang open.

"You... don't like it?" the woman questions.

Suddenly, I realize what this means for my interview, my heart slamming hard within my chest as I spring up from my chair.

"Oh my god," I stammer. "I'm so fucked. What did you do?"

"You told me to clean it up," offers the stylist. "I cut out everything that was dirty. I don't think you've washed your hair for a while, though, so I had to take off a lot."

"What the fuck?" I cry out in utter shock. "You did what?"

"I thought that's what you wanted," the stylist continues.

My breathing is so heavy now that I actually think I might pass out, and I know if I stay in this salon any longer the chances of that happening will grow exponentially. I need to get out of here and figure out what I'm gonna do with myself.

I reach into my purse and pull out more than enough cash to cover the cut, opting to take the high road and pay this woman for her work, regardless of how terrible it might be. I toss the my money on the counter and then head for the door, erupting out onto the street.

I feel like the whole world is spinning around me, my plans completely upended by something that honestly shouldn't have any weight in the first place. This is a fucking *science* job, why does it matter what my haircut looks like?

Still, I know the people interviewing me might not share this same philosophy, and likely don't. Despite the fact they came to prominence by cloning sentient butts, Rubble Labs are known for being fairly conservative.

Close to tears and not knowing what else to do, I pull out my phone and immediately dial my best friend, Morgan. It rings twice before she answers, the sound of her voice immediately putting me just the slightest bit at ease.

"Hey Jenn, what's up?" Morgan questions.

"I'm fucked," I blurt.

"You're fucked?" Morgan repeats back to me.

"It doesn't sound like you care!" I cry out, growing frustrated again.

Morgan can't help but chuckle at this, clearly startled by the fact that someone as typically coolheaded as me could've found themselves in such a whirlwind of emotions.

"I care, I care," Morgan assures me. "What's wrong?"

"I went in to get a haircut before the big Rubble Labs interview," I explain. "It *did not* turn out well."

"Oh no," Morgan groans. "Send me a pic."

I pull my phone away and snap a selfie, then shoot it over to my friend with a quick text message. I put the phone back against my head and wait for her response.

"Holy shit," Morgan suddenly blurts when the message comes through.

"That bad?" I question, already knowing the answer.

"It's… really something," my friend stammers, then straightens up a bit, "but listen, everything's gonna be okay. You should've come to me in the first place, but I can still get you out of this mess."

"You cut hair?" I question.

"No, but I know the best barber in town and she's gonna make sure you're looking your absolute best for this interview," Morgan explains. "She's pretty hard to get and appointment with, though."

"I need this cut *tonight*," I counter. "Do you think she has any openings?"

"Oh no, it's not about openings," Morgan explains. "She's just selective about her clients. She takes her art *very* seriously."

"Well, if she can help me out then I don't care," I counter. "I'll do whatever it takes."

I arrive a half-hour later at the address Morgan gave me, and at first I'm not exactly sure what I'm looking at. It appears to be nothing more than a simple roll up door to an industrial car garage, nobody else around for miles on either side of these dimly lit streets.

I double check that address that Morgan sent me, making sure this is the place, then knock twice on the metal roll up door.

No response.

I stand here for a long while as I start to consider just turning around and calling it a loss, but before I go, I knock one final time.

Suddenly, the roll up door rises with a loud clatter, causing me to jump back in alarm. Standing before me is a beautiful T-Rex with a pair of sheers in her hands, who says absolutely nothing as she eyes me up and down.

"I'm here to see Ralla Brims," I offer. "I was hoping she might have an opening for me."

"You're hair is a disaster," the dinosaur observes, getting right to the point.

"Yeah," I reply with a nod. "It is."

"Do you believe love is real?" Ralla asks me flatly.

I consider her question. "Uh... yes," I finally reply.

"We're closed," the beautiful T-Rex informs me, "but I think we can make an exception in a case this... dramatic."

"Thank you so much," I gush as the dinosaur barber leads me inside. "I'm Jenn."

It's only now that I get a chance to see just how exquisitely crafted this barbershop really is, a state of the art salon with a clean, modern design that makes me feel as though I'm in some kind of luxury spa. I can see why it's so exclusive, especially when I realize there's only one barber's chair in the whole place.

Ralla leads me over and sits me down in the chair, facing me towards a large mirror as she begins to play with what's left of my hair. The beautiful dinosaur runs her short claws through my locks for a moment, getting as sense of me, and without warning this simple touch sends a powerful, erotic chill through my body. Of course, I try my best to keep my thoughts strictly professional, but it's difficult when I'm in such close proximity to such a sensual dinosaur.

"Think you can make me presentable?" I question.

"That depends on what you mean," the dinosaur retorts. "I don't do hair to make you look good in the eyes of someone else. I do hair to make you to look good in the eyes of yourself."

"Isn't that usually the same thing?" I ask.

"Hardly," Ralla replies. The beautiful scaly creature stops running her claws through my hair, narrowing her eyes in a moment of deep seriousness. "If I cut your hair, it's going to be an expression of who you are, not who someone else wants you to be."

"As long as it looks good in an interview, I'm fine," I continue.

The T-Rex shakes her head. "As long as you *feel* good in your interview," she retorts.

I consider this for a moment and then finally agree. "Alright, lets do this."

"Good!" Ralla replies, patting me on the shoulder.

The dinosaur stands up straight and then walks around to the front, standing directly before my chair as she looks me in the eye.

"Is everything alright?" I question.

The beautiful T-Rex nods. "If I'm going to understand your hair, then I need to understand your *body*," she informs me. "It's a very... intimate process."

The second Ralla says this I feel the erotic yearnings within me double in size, spilling out across my veins and filling me with a bubbling, blossoming desire. I can't remember the last time I was this attracted to someone else, and it sounds like intimacy is the key, regardless. If I want to have a haircut that accurately represents the core of my very being, then going emotionally deep is exactly what Ralla and me need to do.

Fortunately, we both appear to be on the same page of this equation.

Slowly, seductively, the beautiful dinosaur begins to strip off her clothes, pulling them away from her scaly body and tossing them to the side. Her prehistoric form is perfectly sculpted, with breathtaking curves the likes of which I've never seen.

A soft whimper escapes my throat when Ralla's green breasts are finally exposed, full and beautiful. The dinosaur moves closer and closer, pushing them up against my body but then lowering herself down. When the prehistoric creature reaches my pants, she carefully takes my fly button in her enormous, sharpened teeth, tearing it away and then sliding the fabric down my body. My panties come next, suddenly leaving me utterly exposed to this ravishing T-Rex.

"First, I need to see what you taste like," the beautiful dinosaur offers.

Ralla gets to work on my pussy, starting slowly as she begins to circle my aching clit with her soft dinosaur tongue. This particular oral muscle of hers is incredible powerful, but she uses it with a great deal of restraint, holding back and taking her time to warm me up. Gradually, the two of us fall into a pleasant groove together, my hips pumping gently against her face as the pleasure within me builds.

Ralla is incredibly good at working me in this way, but despite her flawless technique, I still find myself wanting to pull her closer. I reach my hands down and move her head towards me, causing the pressure against my clit to grow more and more. I spread my legs even wider in the chair, wading into the erotic sensitivity as it becomes almost too much to bear like some mischievous tickle.

"Oh my god, oh my god" I stammer, repeating the words over and over again in a spastic mantra that starts off quiet and grows louder with every passing repetition.

To my amazement, I suddenly realize I could cum at any second, a powerful climax looming above me like a tidal wave that's waiting to crest.

I hang on for as long as I can before giving into this sensation, allowing the climax to erupt across my frame, spilling through my body and sweeping me away in a feast of the senses. I lose myself in this moment, throwing my head back and letting out a startled cry as my muscles expand and contract in unison.

When I finally finish, I find myself even more sexually energized than before. I want to give back in the way I've been so lucky to receive, to allow Ralla the sensations she's so diligently blessed me with.

Stripping away my clothing, I slink out of the chair, crawling across the floor towards the beautiful dinosaur as I gaze up at her with lustful, fuck-me eyes. Once I'm positioned directly below her I immediately dive in, getting to work on her slick pussy with my tongue. I begin to implement the same techniques that the sexy prehistoric hairstylist used on me, starting off slow as I move in careful circles across Ralla's clit.

Over time, I allow myself a little more speed and pressure, swirling at a steady rate while the dinosaur leans back against her barber's table. The dinosaur is moaning softly, bucking her hips along to the movement of my mouth.

Eventually, I slip two fingers deep within her, adding a second sensation to the mix. Now these two sources begin working together in a potent cocktail of ecstasy, building up more and more until it appears Ralla is about to explode. The dinosaur closes her eyes tight, whimpering slightly as I move my fingers and tongue faster and faster until, finally, she erupts with a powerful roar. The prehistoric creature is overwhelmed with orgasmic sensation, shaking hard as she braces herself on the deck behind her.

When Ralla finishes there's a fire in her eyes, the barber more belligerent with lust than ever.

"Now I wanna see what you fuck like," the dinosaur groans, then pulls open her barber's desk, extracting an enormous green strap-on. "Now."

"Please," I beg. "Pound me with that giant strap-on cock."

The sexy dinosaur slips into her toy's harness and turns it on, causing a small vibrating egg to hum loudly within the inner base.

I turn around the crawl back up onto the barber's chair, wiggling my rump from side to side as I go. I reach back and playfully slap my ass, then take one finger and beckon my T-Rex lover towards me.

"What are you waiting for?" I coo. "Fuck me."

Ralla steps up behind me and aligns her rod with the slickness of my pussy, taking her time to get the perfect angle and then sliding forward in a deep, powerful swoop.

I let out a startled yelp as my dinosaur lover enters me, not entirely prepared for the enormity of her strap-on rod. Fortunately, Ralla takes her time, holding fast as she allows my body to adjust.

Soon enough, the tension within me begins to slip away, replaced instead by a potent, aching warmth. I look back over my shoulder at the beautiful dinosaur, nodding when I'm finally ready and then watching as she begins to push in and out of my body with slow, steady assurance. We quickly fall into sync with one another, our frames pulsing together in a way that's both graphically carnal and breathtakingly intimate.

"More," I demand, a fire in my eyes.

Ralla begins to speed up, hammering away at me harder and harder as I give myself back to her completely. I'm loving every second of this, enjoying the way it feels to submit myself to this powerful woman. With one hand, I reach down between my legs and begin to frantically rub my clit, picking a pace that seems to work with Ralla's thrusts from behind.

Soon, that familiar sensation of impending orgasm begins to escalate within me once more, bubbling up to the surface and consuming my nerve endings. Everything within my body feels tense and ready to explode, but in the most glorious of ways.

"I'm so close, I'm so close," I begin to whimper, a phrase that keeps Ralla at exactly the same pace, pounding away at my pussy with feminine confidence.

Suddenly, I realize the building tension within me has stopped, something not quite adding up as I struggle to reach my peak for a second time.

"Wait," I suddenly blurt. "Don't move."

Ralla does as she's told, holding deep inside me as I continue to frantically rub my clit. A smile begins to creep its way across my lips as I realize this is exactly what I needed.

"Just be close to me," I continue.

The beautiful dinosaur leans down behind me, her scaly breasts and stomach pressed hard against my back as we simply exist in each other's presence.

I feel as though a padlock as been opened within my lions, all of these powerful erotic sensations surging through the opening and almost immediately filling my body to the brim. Seconds later, I'm pushing myself over the edge, cumming hard across Ralla's strap-on dick.

"Oh fuck!" I scream, the sound eventually transforming into a long hiss that cascades out through my clenched teeth.

I can sense Ralla clenching up behind me, the inner vibrator of her strap-on simultaneously pushing her over the edge. She pulls me even closer, our bodies wrapped tightly against one another as we experience this powerful sensation in unison.

Finally, we collapse against the chair, breathing heavy as we struggle to collect ourselves. Ralla pulls out of me slowly, then slips off her strap-on. She shuts it down and places the sex toy back in her drawer, pulling out a pair of clippers instead.

"I feel like I know you very, very well now," the dinosaur offers with a smile. "That was a good time."

"Good enough for the perfect cut?" I question.

Ralla nods.

Soon enough, the process begins, Ralla making her way back and forth and working her magic across my head. She takes plenty of time with me, laboring on the cut with a precision and devotion unlike anything I've ever seen. Every once in a while she'll step back to get a full view of what's happening, then quickly dive back in for a few more trims.

The whole while, I find my eyes locked onto the image in the mirror before me. I'm understandably nervous at first, but as my haircut continues along I find myself growing more and more at ease, eventually allowing myself to relax completely.

When the final haircut is revealed I can't help but smile, blown away at just how much Ralla has seemed to capture the inner essence of my personality.

"It looks... amazing," I gush.

The dinosaur barber nods and gives me a playful wink. "I know," she offers in return.

I turn my head from side to side, still admiring her handwork. "It's definitely not conservative, though," I observe. "This is pretty wild for a job interview."

"*You're* pretty wild," Ralla explains. "Sure, it's nice to get cleaned up a bit before something like this, but you still want to show them the best side of *you.*"

"You're right," I reply.

I stand up from the chair as my dinosaur stylist brushes away some hair from my apron, then pulls the whole thing off of me.

"Thank you so much, what do I owe you?" I question.

"Nothing," the gorgeous T-Rex replies. "That was a good time for both of us. Just promise you'll come back next time you need a trim."

Ralla reaches into her drawer once more and pulls out a business card, handing it over. Her number is emblazed boldly across the top.

"You can also just call me to hang out sometime," the beautiful dinosaur continues.

"I think I'll do that," I tell her.

This conference room is utterly silent as the women across the table from me go over my reports, looking intently through page after page of documents that I've prepared. Normally, I'd be consumed by tension right about now, but my fresh new haircut has given me a righteous surge of confidence that simply can't be contained.

The head of this division, a fierce woman named Monica, finally sits back up and removes her reading glasses.

"This is good, really good," Monica informs me. "I can see why you've made it this far in the interview process. You're exactly what we're looking for here at Rubble Labs."

Her praise fills me with a powerful sense of pride and accomplishment. "Thank you," I reply.

"You're hired," the woman continues.

This is a moment I've been working towards my whole life, and now that I'm finally here it feels amazing to be recognized for my tenacity and intelligence.

"There's just one thing," Monica continues, narrowing her eyes a bit. "Your hair cut is a little… wild for this company. We'd like things to be more uniform."

"But, you want to hire *me*, right?" I question.

Monica nods. "You. Without the hair."

I take a deep breath and let it out, suddenly realizing that I'm about to say something I never thought possible. Never in my wildest dreams could I have imagined I'd find myself in this position, and then do what I'm about to do.

Still, it feels absolutely right. There's a very clear path laid out ahead of me, and I'm ready to take it.

"I'm sorry," I finally say, "but I'll have to respectfully decline your offer."

Monica just stares across the table at me blankly, while the women who flank her on either side begin to whisper amongst themselves.

"You're right about one thing, I'm the best candidate for this job. I know biotech inside and out, and I'm already pioneering technologies that are gonna pave the way of the future. As much as I want to work for you, I *also* wanna work for a company that accepts all of me," I explain. "That includes the wild hair cut."

"So you're just… quitting biotech?" Monica clarifies.

"Oh no," I retort, standing up and gathering my things. "I'm gonna work even harder than ever. I'm just going to start my own company."

I turn around and head for the door with utter confidence, excited to see what comes next.

A BUTT IN THE MIST: STIRRED TO THE CORE OF MY BODICE BY THE DUCHESS TRICERATOPS OF HELENA

I knew my life would change when I left for the new world, setting a course across the vast Atlantic Ocean and then further still through the uncharted wilds of America. It was a journey I spent many long nights regretting as I stared up at the ceiling of my horse drawn carriage, the lanterns swinging back and forth as the wooden vessel shook and rattled around me. I wasn't used to these rocky roads, and the trembling of the vehicle made me sick.

Who would've thought I'd end up here, so far away from home and trapped in a land that seemed the absolute opposite of everything I'd trained for. I'd dedicated years of my life to the field of hospitality, hoping to find myself behind the scenes at any one of the most luxurious hotels across England.

But when I finally graduated from my training and went out to find a job, all the positions were filled. I'd worked so hard and suddenly found myself in a world full of clones, men and women who were more than willing to do whatever it took for the job.

Of course, I'm no slacker, and I'm keen to give everything I've got in the name of good service, but I'm also someone who was trained to value poise, tradition and distinction.

With no job prospects in my future, I suddenly began to worry about making ends meet. It seemed like only yesterday that my future was so bright and cheery, the whole world laid out ahead of me. Now, suddenly, I'm wondering if I'll be able to keep a roof over my head. Not a single manor, abbey, or castle had the space for me.

It's only then I learned about the New World Program, which was championed by the Queen herself in an attempt to get things off the ground in America. The program was an important part of the new world expansion, designed to make sure colonization remained focused on the long standing traditions of the glorious land being left behind.

In other words, they wanted us to make sure the grace and elegance of England was being maintained in a place that was otherwise quite wild. We were ambassadors of culture, sent out to run various manors across America with absolute grace and dignity, serving tea and playing croquet should the weather allow.

Finally, I'd found employment, helped mostly by the fact that not many people are ready to commit to traveling halfway across the world with little to no chance of ever coming back. Without any family, I was a perfect candidate, and my youthful excitement and enthusiasm only pushed my application over the top.

Now here I am, in the middle of nowhere with a forest on either side of me that stretches out as far as the eye can see. Of course, here in the late hours of the evening, there's not much of anything to look at beyond the shell of my carriage, just differing shades of darkness that float pass on either side of the road, barely visible in the dancing lamplight.

Supposedly, a small and simple castle by the name of Billings Manor should be out here somewhere, but so far its hard to believe that we'll find much of anything. I'm growing more and more convinced that the driver has just been taking me around the woods in an endless loop for weeks, seeing how long it will take for me to crack.

Gazing out the window of my carriage, however, I suddenly spot the flicker of something yellow as it drifts out through the moving trees.

At first I'm certain my eyes are playing tricks on me, but the closer we get, the more this yellow glow become visible.

"Billings Manor, coming up around the bend!" my drivers cries out, the first new words that I've heard from him in days.

As I watch, the glow grows and transforms, eventually revealing the well manicured grounds of a beautiful castle the likes of which I haven't seen once since leaving my homeland. The carriage continues onward as we make our way past the hedges and gardens, eventually arriving out front where a large circular roundabout has been constructed before the front entryway.

I climb out of the carriage as the driver gathers my things.

"Ms. Allison Davenport I presume," says an older woman as she approaches in the darkness, a maid standing next to her and holding a lantern so that she doesn't have to do it herself.

"That is I," I reply with a nod.

"I'm Mrs. Glibber, the head of Billings Manor," this stone-faced older woman informs me, a stern frown plastered across her face as though it's been chiseled in marble.

"It's so wonderful to make your acquaintance," I offer, extending a hand. "I've been looking forward to my time here at the manor. I have a lot of ideas that could help this place run even more smoothly."

Suddenly, Mrs. Glibber turns her attention to the carriage driver as he unfastens my bags. "No, no," the woman announces loudly. "Allison will take care of her own bags."

The carriage driver stops abruptly, exchanging glances with me before finally stepping away.

I stroll over and unfasten my luggage, groaning loudly as I'm forced to carry down this excruciatingly heavy gear myself.

"You are here to work," Mrs. Glibber says sternly. "I don't know what they told you over in England, but at Billings Manor you are to listen, not speak."

"I'm sorry, I just thought…" I stammer.

"You were wrong," Mrs. Glibber interrupts. "The help we need here at Billings Manor is physical, not intellectual. I don't care what you *think* will improve the operations around here, because we don't have the time."

"Why not?" I question.

"Because The Duchess Triceratops Of Helena is coming to visit in two days, and it's up to us to make a good impression," Mrs. Glibber informs me.

I open my mouth to say something but before I can, the woman has turned around and is walking back towards the castle, the lantern carrier hustling along beside her.

I'm left in the darkness with my heavy bags as the carriage pulls away, the cold and unfamiliar air of this new world enveloping me. I take a deep breath and let it out, accepting the choices that I've made to lead me here, and then use all the strength I can muster to carry my luggage up the steps of this enormous castle.

Over the next few days I begin to settle into the routine of the manor, and quickly discover the nuances of Mrs. Glibber's brutal rule. Everyone who works here lives in fear of the angry women, terrified we'll do something to displease her and cause her to immediately toss us out in the cold.

We are tasked with so much to do here that the prospect of early unemployment isn't so bad on the surface, but when you consider that fact there's nowhere to go for hundreds of miles, it actually becomes a little dangerous. Besides, what else am I going to do with all of this training in manners and elegance?

Fortunately, the whirlwind of activity here at Billings Manor has kept my profile low, allowing me to blend in amid the hustle and bustle. Mrs. Glibber is squarely focused on making this visit with The Duchess Triceratops Of Helena go smoothly, and so long as an action doesn't directly impede this desire, it generally goes unnoticed.

As the time draws nearer, however, tensions begin to rise.

It quickly becomes apparent that, because Mrs. Glibber runs this place with an iron fist, she doesn't have many friends around to fill out the space of the manor, leaving it cold and empty. All of us with training in manners have been relegated to the kitchen or the laundry room.

It's no surprise when Mrs. Glibber suddenly comes bursting into the servant's quarters to see me.

"Allison," she begins, trying her best to hide her desperation. "I need your help with dinner."

"I know, madam," I reply with a nod. "I'll be in the kitchen making sure everything goes as planned."

Mrs. Glibber shakes her head. "No, I mean, I need you at the table."

My heart skips a beat when I hear this, suddenly realizing what's going on.

"You want me to entertain?" I question.

Mrs. Glibber shakes her head. "No, no. In fact, I don't want you to say a word while the duchess and I talk. You'll be there to fill the space and make this manor look lively and fun."

"Are you sure you wouldn't like me to *talk* with The Duchess Triceratops Of Helena?" I continue prodding, "because I've been trained in this kind of thing. I'm an expert conversationalist."

Mrs. Glibber's expression suddenly changes as she marches towards me, overflowing with a seething rage the likes of which I've never seen. Her sudden movement causes me to stumble back a bit, staggering until I slam into the wall behind me then cowering in fear as the woman pushes in farther and farther. Now she's mere centimeters from my face.

"Don't you dare say a word," Mrs. Glibber commands, her eyes alight with anger. "If I hear a single peep from you during the course of this dinner, then I'll be eating *you* from breakfast. Understood?"

It takes a moment for me to collect myself, at which point I finally nod in acceptance. "Yes. Understood."

"Good," Mrs. Glibber hisses before turning around and storming out of the kitchen. She stops in the doorway, then turns around to face me once more. "Come on. She'll be here any minute."

I spring into action, desperately collecting myself as I fall into step behind the woman.

The next thing I know, we're rushing down the stonework halls of the manor, twisting and turning through the building until we arrive at the dining room.

"There," Mrs. Glibber commands. "Sit near us at the head of the table."

I see now the rest of the seats are taken by various servants done up to look like royalty. They exchange glances awkwardly as I enter the room and take one of the few empty chairs left. Meanwhile, Mrs. Glibber continues onward to the front of the castle where she'll soon be greeting The Duchess Triceratops Of Helena's carriage.

I take a deep breath and let it out, trying my best to mentally prepare for the dinner to come. My instructions are simple, to simply exist here without saying a word, but for some reason I get the feeling this might prove to be difficult.

My eyes stay transfixed on the door before me as the tension in the room builds, an anxious ache that spills out through my bloodstream and looms larger and larger over my psyche.

Suddenly, Mrs. Glibber and The Duchess Triceratops Of Helena emerge, stepping into the dining room in a fit of boisterous laughter. It becomes clear very quickly, however, that Mrs. Glibber is the only one laughing. The duchess, on the other hand, seems downright exhausted.

This is the first time I've ever seen The Duchess Triceratops Of Helena, and it's abundantly clear that the rumors of her beauty were not exaggerated in the slightest. The woman is a stunning prehistoric creature with three ivory white horns atop her scaly green head. Her mouth is perfectly shaped into a powerful beak, and you can tell that her body is also curved in all the right places despite the many ornate and royal fabrics that cover her up.

Mrs. Glibber sits right next to me while the gorgeous triceratops sits across, the dinosaur clearly doing her best to seem interested but faltering slightly. At this point I'm not even sure Mrs. Glibber notices, but my social training has taught me to pick up on the slightest cues that might otherwise go unseen. The triceratops is glancing around the room for something interesting to look at, nodding along as Mrs. Glibber blathers about the history of this manor and the improvements they've been making to the luxurious structure.

My immediate impulse is to jump in and help steer things in a new direction, to save this ship before it sinks below the surface and can never be returned. I'm forced to hold back, however, biting my tongue and following my strict orders.

I have to admit, this is harder than I thought, not simply due to this awkward situation, but thanks to the fact that there's something undeniably attractive about The Duchess Triceratops Of Helena. Her scales shimmer in the lamplight, flickering and dancing in a way that's absolutely mesmerizing. I find myself drawn to her like a powerful, erotic spell, a spell that's only elevated by the fact it's so taboo and forbidden.

"And the North garden also has some wonderful flowers in the springtime," Mrs. Glibber drones. "Every color you could imagine: red… yellow… blue… green… white… black… pink."

Finally, the duchess has had enough, turning towards me and smiling wide. "And what do *you* think of the garden?"

I just stare at the triceratops like a rabbit in a trap, not quite sure how to react to her question. My eyes begin to dart between this beautiful dinosaur and my new boss, who has given me very specific instructions of utter silence.

Mrs. Glibber's eyes are wide as she stares daggers into me, clearly pressuring me to refrain from a response.

Finally, the dinosaur duchess turns her attention to Mrs. Glibber. "Can she not speak?"

"Afraid not," Mrs. Glibber replies. "None of them can."

The Duchess Triceratops Of Helena narrows her eyes, suddenly skeptical of this. "Not a single person here.... besides yourself... is capable of speech?"

Mrs. Glibber now realizes how bizarre this sounds but pushes onward with her lie, doubling down. "I'm afraid not. There was a terrible accident when the manor was under construction. Fortunately, I was away on business, but the entire staff was rendered silent."

Suddenly, the head chef of the castle bursts through the kitchen door holding a tray of immaculately crafted appetizers, a sizzling selection of the manor's finest dishes.

"Sorry to keep you waiting!" the head chef announces, placing the tray between Mrs. Glibber and our triceratops guest.   The chef then abruptly turns and heads back into the kitchen.

"So not everyone is silent," the duchess clarifies.

At this point, the aching frustration within me has finally grown to a breaking point. I'm sick of following these inane rules for no reason other than to please Mrs. Glibber. Who cares if I'll be thrown out into the forest? I'd rather be there then continue to serve here under such a horrible leader.

"I'm not," I finally announce.

Mrs. Glibber's eyes go wide with anger but she says nothing in protest, not wanting to dig herself into an even deeper hole.

"Oh really!" the duchess replies, turning her attention to me once more. "That's great, because you seem very interesting and I'd like to get to know you more."

There's something about the way the beautiful dinosaur says this that sends a powerful chill down my spine. There is clearly a weight behind her words, a double meaning as she smiles with her perfectly curved triceratops beak.

"What's your name?" the dinosaur questions.

"Allison," I reply.

The prehistoric creature nods as she listens. "Very good. I'm The Duchess Triceratops Of Helena, but you may call me Sarah."

Suddenly, Mrs. Glibber interjects. "Can *I* call you Sarah?"

"No you may not," the dinosaur replies swiftly.

Sarah reaches across the table and places a scaly hand upon mine.

"Would you like to join me for a night walk in the garden? I'd much rather see it for myself than talk and talk and talk about what it's like. It's getting a little stuffy in here, anyway."

"Of course," I reply, my voice trembling with erotic anticipation.

"Good!" retorts the dinosaur, standing abruptly. "I'll meet you down there in fifteen minutes."

Mrs. Glibber flashes a venomous grin, clearly excited to take her anger out on me the second Sarah leaves.

"And if anything happens to her," the triceratops continues. "I will know who to come looking for. Is that understood, Mrs. Glibber?"

My boss leans back into her chair once more, defeated.

The silence of the forest is overwhelming as I step out into the garden courtyard, an enormous yellow moon hanging above me. Unfortunately, a low fog has rolled in, obscuring the stars and covering the ground with a swirling mist, but this also adds to the sense of danger and mystery.

"Hello?" I call out, not too loudly as I don't want to bother the other castle workers who may be sleeping in their quarters nearby. "Are you out here, Sarah?"

No response.

I creep into the mist, my eyes adjusting to the darkness of the garden as I peer into the strange, swirling landscape. For a moment I think I've caught a glimpse of her, but then seconds later I realize the figure is nothing more than a stone statue wrapped with ivy.

Deeper and deeper I push into the garden until, suddenly, I stop. I slight gasp escapes my throat, not from fear, but from powerful erotic intrigue.

There before me is the glorious silhouette of Sarah's dinosaur form, swaying her hips from side to side and completely nude. The only thing I can make out for sure is the gentle curve of her gorgeous green butt.

Second's later, the rump disappears.

I pick up my pace, following The Duchess Triceratops Of Helena deeper into the fog but immediately losing track of her.

"Where are you?" I cry out, not knowing where to turn.

Suddenly, the beautiful dinosaur seems to appear directly behind me. I swirl around and embrace her, pulling the beautiful creature close and then kissing her passionately on the beak. The two of us immediately explode in a fit of passion, our hands exploring one another's bodies as she strips away my clothing, tossing it to the side.

I shiver in the cool night air, a tingling sensation pulsing across my skin as my triceratops lover runs her hand slowly down my shoulder and then across my breasts. She teases me for a moment and I return the favor, taking things even further as I allow my attention to slip lower and lower across her breathtaking form.

Soon enough, I'm playfully running my fingertips across her waistline, threatening to dip below.

"Please," the triceratops begs, the single word whispered into my ear.

I have mercy, reaching down and beginning to circle my finger gently across her wet clit. Immediately, Sarah reacts, sighing loudly as she pushes her body even harder against mine. She begins to move along with my hand, grinding hard as the two of us passionately kiss once more.

I can see The Duchess Triceratops Of Helena's hand creeping closer towards me, hoping to return the favor, but before she gets a chance I drop to my knees. I appreciate the give and take, but right now I'm desperately in the mood to please.

I gaze up at Sarah with lustful eyes then dive into her dinosaur pussy, flicking my tongue to the same rhythm as my fingers before it. I start lightly enough and then gradually begin to use more and more force, working her to the natural movements of her body. Above me, the beautiful triceratops begins to groan loudly, placing her hands on the back of my head and running her fingers through my hair.

It's not long before Sarah begins to tremble and quake, the first hints of orgasm beginning to work their way out across her prehistoric body. The muscles of her stomach are clenched tight, aching for release but only building and building with carnal tension.

"Oh fuck, oh fuck, oh fuck," The Duchess Triceratops Of Helena repeats under her breath, the mantra growing louder with every passing repetition. "Oh fuck, oh fuck!"

I can sense she's just about to reach her limit, and at this very moment I slip two fingers within her, never letting up for a second with my tongue. Immediately, Sarah erupts in a fit of prehistoric climax, losing herself in the moment as she throws her head back and lets out a powerful triceratops roar. Her entire body is shaking and, for a moment, I worry she might actually buckle at the knees. Somehow, she manages to stay upright.

Once Sarah finally finishes, however, she drops down next to me, crawling over my body as she pushes me back against the soft garden grass. Our nude forms are now intertwined in a pretzel of passion, hands and fingers working their way across one another.

Lower and lower the beautiful triceratops begins to explore, stopping at my belly button as she gazes up at me with eyes that overflow with lust and, maybe, something more. Dispute the fact this interaction is clearly one of physical passion, I'd be lying if I didn't admit to the mighty, mystical draw this triceratops has over me. I haven't had much time to consider the meaning of our connection, but the *feeling* of it is something that I've never before experienced. I've spent my whole life learning how to fit into a complicated system of manners and customs, never really considering what it might be like to break out of them. In this moment with Sarah, I finally feel completely free to be myself, to act in the ways that my body desires at its very core.

The Duchess Triceratops Of Helena creeps lower still, finally arriving at my pussy. She immediately gets to work, running her tongue slowly across my clit in a series of long, drawn out movements. Steadily, the triceratops gains momentum, taking careful note of the ways I'm reacting to her touch. The sensation is incredible, not just because she clearly knows how to eat a woman out, but because she's paying close attention to the specifics of my body. I can tell the triceratops is making a mental note of every whimper and sigh that I make, adjusting her technique in subtle ways as she carries me along with her.

Meanwhile, I can feel Sarah's large triceratops finger teasing the lips of my pussy, letting me know that she's there. I begin to nod furiously as I continue to sigh and squirm, letting her know that I want it.

Moment's later, I feel Sarah's finger slip within my tightness, filling me up as a startled groan escapes my lips.

"Oh my god, you're gonna make me cum so fucking hard," I admit, my face flushed and my heart hammering within my chest.

The Duchess Triceratops Of Helena stays the course, continuing to work me as the wave of climax looms higher and higher above, threatening to break at any moment. When it finally does, I do everything I can to let it sweep me away, to keep myself from pushing back against the incredible surge of pleasure that washes through my form.

I tilt my head back and let out a long, powerful scream, my voice carrying through the misty night and echoing across the forest beyond. I feel like I'm one with the wilds now, free from any ridiculous rules that had ever bound me.

When I finally finish, I fall back against the grass in complete exhaustion, smiling warmly as the beautiful triceratops crawls up next to me. The two of us cuddle together, enjoying the simple pleasure of skin against scale.

"That was amazing," I gush.

"It was," Sarah agrees, kissing me on the cheek.

"I should really get back inside before I make Mrs. Glibber any more upset than she already is," I continue.

My prehistoric lover laughs. "She doesn't really have a say," Sarah offers. "She may rule *this manor*, but a duchess rules the county."

"Once you leave I'll have to face the music," I explain. "I appreciate what you're saying, but the second your carriage disappears around the bend there will be hell to pay."

"Who says I'm leaving," Sarah replies with a smile, settling in next to me as we gaze up at the luminous moon above.

MY LIBRARIAN IS A BEAUTIFUL LESBIAN ICE CREAM CONE AND SHE TASTES AMAZING

In the modern age, not a lot of people still use the library. Honestly, it's a real shame things have changed in this way, and while I typically welcome new technology with open arms, the ease of the internet has not been entirely kind to the world of paper books.

Of course, libraries have done a lot to change with the times, carving out more space for computer labs and offering ebooks for download. It's not nearly as massive an exodus as it could've been, but it would be crazy to completely ignore the significant drop in attendance.

I, on the other hand, still love the library. As a women who works from home, I appreciate the fact there's a free, public space for me to go and focus. It's quiet and comfortable, with fast wireless internet and basically any office resources I could ever need. I'm not there every single day, but I usually drive over two of three times a week to break up my work habits.

By now, the downtown public library is like a home away from home, a comfortable and welcoming place where my imagination is free to run wild, but when I walk through the doors on this particular afternoon I immediately recognize something is off.

The difference is so subtle that, at first, I'm not exactly sure what it is. Everything around me looks the same, with the same rows of books stretching out in either direction and that same line of worktables positioned directly before me. However, I know at the core of my being that something is amiss.

As I'm thinking about this I can feel a shiver run across my body, causing my exposed skin to tingle ever so slightly. It's only then that I realize what has happened: the temperature within the library is quite a bit lower than I'm used to. On a warm summers day this might be a welcome change, but the weather hasn't been exceptionally hot lately and there's really no reason for this crispness.

The change, however, is not *that* bad. I'm not actively shivering or trying to cover myself up with layers of warm blankets.

I quickly recover, collecting my senses and heading out into the library, briskly walking past the rows and rows of empty worktables to find myself a seat. I pull out a chair at a great spot near the window, then retrieve my laptop computer, diving in.

The longer I'm here, however, the more annoyed I start to get. Is it really that difficult to bump up the temperature to a normal setting? Who decided to make this change, anyway?

Before I have a chance to really get started, I've found my mind flooded with all kinds of irritated thoughts, the frustration piling up inside me until, eventually, I just can't take it anymore. I have to say something.

Frustrated, I put away my laptop and pick up my bag, heading directly towards the library front desk. I know I'm supposed to be quiet, but I can't help calling out a bit before I get there.

"Hey, is there a reason the temperature is so low?" I question. "I'm trying to get some work done and it's actually a little distracting."

I round the corner and arrive at the front desk, suddenly finding myself face to face with an unexpected sight. There before me is a librarian that I haven't yet met, a new hire who just happens to be an enormous sentient ice cream cone.

"Oh," I stammer, knocked back a bit when I see her.

It's not that I've never encountered a sentient ice cream cone before, more the fact that I've never seen one this breathtakingly gorgeous. She's absolutely stunning, with two distinct scoops of flavor in a golden waffle cone body that tapers down in just the right way. She's also incredibly well put together, not a single drip running along either side of her sugary body.

The ice cream cone is cataloging some books when I approach her, deeply focused but pulling away from her duties to help me out.

"Hey there," the chilled dessert offers with a smile.

"Hi," is all I can think to say, trying my best to gather my thoughts. "I just… I wanted to know why it's so cold in here."

The ice cream cone falters slightly. I can tell this is a sore subject. "I'm sorry about that," she replies. "I'm new here and, well, we had to bump the temperature down a little to keep me from melting. I wasn't sure if anyone would notice just a few degrees, but it's been causing some problems today."

I glance around the library, realizing now the emptiness on this particular afternoon is not just random chance.

"It's not a big deal," I reply, trying to make the best of the situation. "I was just curious."

"I'll let the head librarian know," continues the gorgeous living dessert.

"Oh no, it's fine," I offer, changing course. "Don't worry about it."

The ice cream cone sighs. "I really *should* pass the complaint along, though. I'm here to help, you know? If there's a problem with the way I'm doing my job then I'm not gonna hide that."

I admire her sense of honor, despite the fact I wouldn't do the same if I was in her shoes. In this moment, I'm suddenly hit with an even more powerful wave of admiration, only this time I begin to understand it for what it really is, lustful attraction.

Of course, who wouldn't be attracted to an ice cream cone this beautiful and kind.

"Is there anything else I can help you with?" the dessert suddenly questions, breaking through my trance.

I realize now that I'd been staring through her, completely spaced out as I drift in an ocean of fantasy.

"Oh, no," I stammer. "Sorry about that."

"What's your name?" the chilled treat suddenly questions, a twinkle of interest in her eye.

"I'm Sally," I inform her.

"Drenda," replies the ice cream cone. "It's really, *really* nice to meet you."

We stand here awkwardly for a moment until, finally, I turn back around and return to my table. The lower temperature is still something of a bother, but Drenda seems especially kind and I'm willing to give this slight change a shot. Tomorrow, I'll just wear a sweater.

I sit at my table by the window and pull out my laptop, opening it up and then diving into my work. I takes a minute for me to stop thinking about the cold air that dances across my exposed skin, but eventually these thoughts fade into the background of my mind. Soon enough, I'm hammering away at the keys before me, taking down a variety of work tasks at a lightening quick pace.

I barely notice as my to-do list gets shorter and shorter, until suddenly I look up and realize that I'm almost completely finished.

"Wait… What?" is all I can think to blurt, the words falling out of my mouth in astonishment.

I vaguely remember an article I'd once read about workflow in colder temperatures, how people are likely to be much more productive when the thermostat is turned down just a few degrees.

"This is amazing," I sigh to myself, double-checking to make sure I didn't actually just forget a few of my daily tasks. Instead, I discover I've taken care of both today and *tomorrow's* workload.

Immediately, I start to pack up my things, excited to return to the front desk and tell my new friend about this incredible discovery. While it had seemed a little annoying at first, this slight temperature change has multiplied my productivity two fold. I've gotta start coming to the library more often.

I approach the desk with a smile on my face, excited to tell Drenda the good news and hoping to flirt a little more, but I suddenly find myself faced with the unexpected scowl of head librarian, Manti Shims.

As I've said plenty of times now, I love coming here to work, but Manti's the one thing that's a consistent disappointment about my visits. Her attitude is terrible, apparently existing in a constant state of annoyance and arrogant dismissal.

"Where did Drenda go?" I question.

"Who?" Manti replies firmly.

"That ice cream cone that just started working here," I continue.

"Oh, yes," Drenda replies, letting out a long sigh. "I had to let her go. We were getting too many complaints about the temperature and it just wasn't a good fit."

I'm not quite sure how to react to this news, startled by the speed at which all this has transpired, but also finding myself slightly sympathetic to Manti's plight. The library is a place where people want to be comfortable, so what was she supposed to do?

Of course, it's also a place for the whole community to come and learn, ice cream and human alike.

Most importantly, I find my mind transfixed on a single, horrifying fact: that I may never see that beautiful sentient dessert again. I know our time together was short, but the attraction I felt for Drenda was strong enough to be followed up on.

"Do you know where she went?" I question.

"Home," replies the head librarian.

"No, I mean, where's home?" I continue.

Manti shrugs. "I think she lives down by the docks in one of those warehouses. There are pretty big freezers around those parts."

"Thanks," I reply, then take off in search of Drenda.

When I find her, I'm not exactly sure what I'll say, but the compulsion is just too strong to ignore.

While I appreciate Manti's hint that the beautiful ice cream might be living by the docks, her directions could hardly be seen as narrowing things down. There's a countless number of warehouses down here, ranging from empty and abandoned to hustling, bustling business operations.

I've made my way through about half of them when I'm forced to finally sit down and take a break, my breathing heavy and my heart slamming hard in my chest. This is a lot of work, much more than I anticipated, yet still I'm driven to push onward in my search for that gorgeous sentient ice cream and her cool, collected smile.

It's crazy, I know, but for some reason I keep finding the will to continue my journey.

After a few minutes I stand up to continue my trek when I'm abruptly stopped in my tracks, my eyes focused on something strange that rests a mere five feet from where I was sitting. There before me is a small, melted dollop of ice cream, the drip now transforming into a sugary puddle in the dying sun.

I glance around, checking the nearby warehouses for any signs of life and then gasping slightly when I notice one of them has a door cracked open to the outside world. Immediately, I jog over to the open door and peer inside as a wave of cold air washes across my face.

I glance around in amazement, taking in the beautifully furnished home that has been constructed inside what I now realize is an enormous, industrial sized freezer.

"Hello?" I call out, my voice echoing through the crisp air.

"Coming!" someone cries in return.

There's a moment of shuffling from somewhere within and then, seconds later, the familiar golden cone and two heaping scoops of Drenda come floating around the corner. She stops when she sees me, an unfiltered grin quickly exploding across her face

"Oh my god," the dessert cries out with excitement. "You're the girl from the library! Sally! What are you doing here?"

This is a great question, one I don't quite have a perfect answer to without embarrassing myself.

"I just… wanted to say that I think it's really stupid the way they fired you," I stammer. "I found out and I had to come say something."

Drenda lets out a long sigh and then shrugs in acceptance. "I've gotta stay cold. I understand how that can be a little annoying."

To be honest, I'd been so enraptured by the beautiful living ice cream, I hadn't even noticed how icy it was in her freezer home.

"I was great, actually," I explain. "I got twice as much done as I normally would. The cold made me *way* more productive."

The sentient dessert smiles. "Well, that's really good to know, and I appreciate you saying something. Unfortunately, everyone else didn't really give it a chance."

"Maybe they will!" I counter. "We can go back and talk to Manti about keeping a portion of the library cool enough for you to work there. It can be a special work zone or something like that."

Drenda nods along with me, trying to keep from getting too excited but clearly liking my idea.

"If there's one thing I know about libraries, it's that they belong to everyone. Just because physical books aren't as popular as they once were, doesn't mean libraries can't be an important meeting place for the community. Part of that is making some adjustments so everyone, warm or cold, can enjoy!"

"You're right," Drenda finally agrees with a smile.

"Then let's go get your job back," I cry with excitement.

"Not so fast," the beautiful ice cream retorts. "I've gotta finish this book and *then* maybe we can go. Don't worry, it's really short."

I notice now that Drenda has been holding a thin paperback in her hand, and that behind her is a home absolutely covered by stacks of books. She clearly enjoys reading, and respects the story enough to wait until her tale is done before taking action.

"Are you sure you don't want to just go now?" I question. "Strike while the iron's hot? I'm kinda pumped up."

"Me too," explains Drenda, but first I think it's important to see if it's worth the effort.

"What do you mean?" I question.

The living ice cream holds up her book, revealing the title.

"My Librarian Is A Beautiful Lesbian Ice Cream Cone And She Tastes Amazing," I read aloud. "Wait a minute... is that..."

"About us?" Drenda offers. "It is, actually."

"Who wrote it?" I continue in complete astonishment.

"Chuck Tingle," Drenda explains. "He's writing it as we speak. I've been reading this story for a while now and it's just kicking into gear. I was hoping something meta like this would happen."

"Wait a minute," I counter, shaking my head. "If you're reading all this in a book then why were you surprised when I showed up here?"

"I was faking it," Drenda says with a laugh. "Just trying to play along."

"This is just too crazy," I retort, shaking my head from side to side. "I don't believe you."

With this, the living ice cream cone floats over to me and shows me the page she's on, pointing to a particular sentence.

"This is just too crazy, I retort," I read aloud. "Shaking my head from side to side. I don't believe you."

I stagger back a bit, blown away by this revelation. "Oh my god."

"It's a lot to take in, I know," Drenda continues, gazing down as she flips to the end of the book and reads. "Hmm," she offers, repeating the sound to herself over and over again. Eventually, she breaks out into a fit of laughter.

"What is it?" I question.

"Don't worry," Drenda replies. "It's a happy ending."

I take a deep breath and let it out, trying my best to come to terms with this startling revelation. "What kind of book is this?" I finally ask.

The living ice cream cone offers me a playful wink in return. "You know what kind of book this is. You've known since you met me at the library," she coos. "Don't try and pretend you didn't feel it, too."

I understand exactly what she's talking about, but this whole encounter is still too surreal to admit to myself. There must be a reasonable explanation.

"There's not," Drenda offers.

"Wait, did I say that out loud?" I question.

The living ice cream cone points to the page before her. "Nope, I just read it right here."

Suddenly, the wild and crazy reality of this situation hits me like a wave, almost knocking me over but somehow keeping me upright as my mind reels. I'm nothing but a character in a book, and I'm here for a very specific reason.

"Listen, I might as well tell you, we're not gonna get back into the library by talking to Manti," Drenda explains. "She's just not interested in working with me on this. There's only *one way* for me to return to the library now."

"How's that?" I ask, no idea where this is headed.

"By making this book as good as it can be," explains the sexy living ice cream. "This *very book* is how we'll get inside, and then me and you will be together forever on the self."

I have to admit, that sounds really nice.

"But, how do we make this book great?" I question, my voice trembling slightly.

"Well, this *is* lesbian erotica," coos Drenda in return, swaying from side to side as she floats towards me. "So a little passion couldn't hurt."

The second our bodies meet, Drenda and I are kissing fervently, our hands gracefully exploring one another's beautiful, feminine forms. I let out a long, aching sigh as Drenda touches me, her hands moving across my breasts and then pulling my clothing away. I slowly grow more and more exposed, but as my nude form is revealed the unpleasant chill is nowhere to be found. It's as thought the erotic heat of this moment has warmed me well beyond any icy counter that the world could throw my way.

Soon enough, I'm completely stripped down before the perfectly sculpted ice cream cone, the curves of my nude form on complete display. Drenda takes me in, eyeing me up and down and then grinning wryly. "You're beautiful," the sentient dessert tells me. "You're absolutely perfect."

"You don't mean that," I counter bashfully.

"You'll see," the beautiful ice cream replies, then begins to push me back.

I follow her movements across the room, eventually collapsing back into a leather chair behind me and sinking into the soft cushion. Drenda floats down into position before my body, gazing up with hungry eyes as she pushes my legs open to either side.

The ice cream cone reaches up and begins to rub her finger gently across my aching clit, moving in a slow circle across my most sensitive area. I bite my lip as she touches me, closing my eyes and settling in while my new lover works her magic. I begin to pump my hips along to Drenda's movements, finding a pace as she gets me off.

Eventually, the beautiful ice cream cone takes things even further, leaning in and adding her tongue to the mix. The second she licks across my clit I let a startled gasp escape my throat, not entirely prepared for just how good it would feel to enjoy her coolness. Drenda immediately gets to work, circling my most sensitive area in the same manner that her fingers had just moments earlier. Gradually, she elevates her speed, until eventually she's flicking her tongue across me like a powerful vibration.

"Oh my fucking god, that feels so food," I groan, leaning my head back and gripping tight onto the armrests of the chair below. My first instinct is to bring my legs together and escape these powerful sensations that pulse through my body, but instead I decide to accept them. I open my legs even wider and take it all.

It's not long before I can feel the first hints of orgasm starting to build up within me, spilling out across my veins like a potent erotic potion. I'm shaking, my muscles pulled tight and waiting for release as Drenda drives me closer and closer to the edge.

"Just like that, just like that," I repeat over and over again. I reach down and place my hand on the back of the living ice cream cone's head, pushing her even harder against my pussy.

Without skipping a beat, Drenda slips two fingers within me, and the next thing I know I'm cumming hard, pumping my body against her as the climax floods through in a mighty wave. I let out a frantic scream that fills the icy room and echoes back towards me.

This blissful moment seems to go on and on, lasting an eternity and then simply ending with a resounding thud. I feel absolutely incredible, fucked silly and satisfied, yet I still know this encounter is only just beginning. Now, it's Drenda's turn.

I start to climb down off of my chair but I quickly see that Drenda has other ideas about how I should pleasure her. Instead of letting me move, the sentient dessert climbs up onto the leather furniture, hovering above me as she lowers herself down onto my hungry mouth.

I can see her beautiful pussy at the base of her cone, drifting closer and closer until it's directly upon my lips. I begin to lick, dragging my tongue across her wetness in a series of satisfying movements.

"Earl Grey," I pull away to observe for a moment, "and pistachio."

Drenda smiles, gazing down at me lovingly. "You like?"

"You taste fantastic," I inform her.

I move back into position and then begin to eat her out once more, starting slow as I run my tongue in circles around her swollen clit. I take note of the way she's reacting to me, observing the gentle heaves of her sugary body as she pumps up and down across my face. Clearly she's enjoying herself, but to take her all the way I need to stay focused.

We continue like this for a good while, and soon enough we fall into a perfect rhythm with one another, our bodies practically melting into a single entity. While I lick Drenda's pussy I also begin to touch myself in unison, edging closer and closer to a second orgasm. I move my fingers in time with the lapping of my tongue, trembling and quaking in the same way that the sentient ice cream cone does above me.

"Holy shit, you're gonna make me cum so fucking hard," Drenda announces, bucking wildly against my face.

I keep doing exactly what I'm doing, and moments later the sentient dessert is crumpling forward as her body is overcome with pleasure. At the same time, I get myself off for in an erotic encore of sensation, both me and Drenda completely lost in the moment.

When Drenda's finished she turns around and slides down into my lap, lying against me as we enjoy one another's presence.

"That was incredible," I tell her. "Do you think it's good enough to get us shelved in a library?"

"Well, erotica is a hard sell for that kind of thing," the living ice cream cone explains, "but... maybe someday."

We sit is silence for a moment, wondering what could eventually become of us. Drenda seems to understand all of this meta reality mumbo jumbo more than I do, but even I know that our story is about to come to an end. It's a frightening feeling, but also one that's full of amazement and wonder.

It's not like we'll just disappear completely, though. In fact, if we do happen to get filed away in some library somewhere, we'll probably keep getting checked out for years.

"I know our time is limited, so I guess I'll just say it," Drenda offers. "I love you."

"I love you, too," I tell her.

At Manti's library in downtown Billings, the head librarian closes her book. She's surprised by how much she actually enjoyed something but the notorious author, Dr. Chuck Tingle. It was a little much, at times, but overall it seems like the message was a good one, and it was certainly told in a unique way.

Manti closes the book, titled My Librarian Is A Beautiful Lesbian Ice Cream Cone And She Tastes Amazing, and puts it back on the shelf, then sits for a moment in silence.

Is it really true dropping the temperature a tiny amount can make people slightly more productive? That type if thing is probably not for everyone, but I'm sure a few of the patrons here would enjoy a slightly colder room to work in.

Manti decides to spend the rest of the day figuring out how to make one room in the library a little cooler for anyone who needs it.

MOBY BUTT

Call me horny.

Standing out here on the deck of our vessel, I wish that I could feel the calm my shipmates often describe. Yes, the water is endless and smooth, something that others might find relaxing in a meditative way, but to me it's nature only brings anxiety and torment.

That big beautiful butt is still out there, still swimming away from me while I follow behind. I shall follow that butt to the ends of the earth, but if the sea is infinite, then will I chase for eternity.

This question tumbles through my mind like a whirlpool, repeating over and over again as it sucks me closer to the icy black center. What lies below I do not know, nor do I intend to find out, of course. I plan on reaching Moby Butt someday, of kissing her passionately while she returns the favor, finally connecting in a moment of passion that was promised so many years ago.

This erotic game started as nothing more than a playful attempt to spice things up. My lover, the great Moby Butt, offered to tease me until I couldn't take it any longer, swimming ahead while I followed behind on my enormous sailing vessel. It sounded fun at the time, like a great way to turn things around in the bedroom, and I only expected our little journey to last a few hours.

That was seven years ago.

Now, the sea has warped and changed me, turned me into a ruthless shadow of my former self as I continue the quest. Every time I feel like turning around, I'll catch a glimpse of that enormous sentient butt as she pops her head above the water, teasing me playfully before diving back down again.

Of course, when this game began the two of us went over our safe word, and I still remember it well. I could easily call out to Moby Butt and let her know that the fun is over, that this fetish of longing has run its course and we should get back to the way things used to be. At that very moment this whole thing would be finished, our journey coming to an end while the crew breathes a sigh of relief.

But I just can't bring myself to do it, can't let these magic word travel any farther than the tip of my tongue. If I end the quest now, then what has this all been about? What have the endless nights of longing and yearning been for?

No, I must allow this fantasy to reach its conclusion, whatever that may be, and however tragic the cost.

I take a deep breath and let it out, allowing the sea air to flood my nostrils. It's dawn, and the sun has only just started to crest over the distant, shimmering horizon. The rest of the crew are all down below, sleeping the night away while their captain continues to keep watch.

Who knows, maybe I'll be lucky enough to catch a glimpse of that damn butt.

I stare at the water, looking for any ripple in the waves that could signal Moby Butt's return. Nothing comes. The ass is only here in my thoughts, still taunting me from somewhere far, far away.

Suddenly, I hear a sharp whistle from across the sea, the sound echoing through my ears and causing my eyes to open wide with excitement. I spin around, realizing now that the source of this alert laid well behind me.

"Hark! Is that the round butt I have sought these seven long years?" I cry, running to the other side of the ship and gazing across the water.

The enormous butt rises in the distance, waving to me playfully. "Hey, Captain Amber! You wanna come kiss me?"

"Yes! I do!" I cry out.

"Well, you can if you catch me!" the giant butt continues to tease, her playful giggling carrying out across the mirrorlike ocean of the morning. "I'll let you do anything you want if you just catch me, Captain!"

Moby Butt winks and then dives back down below the water, moving quickly away from the ship.

"The great round butt!" I cry out, running over to a large bell and ringing it to wake the crew. "I've seen the great round butt on the starboard side!"

Almost immediately, I can hear shouting and thundering footsteps from below. Moment's later the crew erupts onto the deck with me, some of them rushing to the edge of the ship while others begin to turn the sail and plot a new course.

"Where is she?" my first mate, Izzy, questions. She's gazing out across the water with her hand over her eyes, trying to see if she can pick up on and irregularity in the waves.

"Right over there!" I scream, pointing as I lean out across the rail, a fire in my eyes.

"Where Captain Amber?" Izzy questions again in earnest.

"She's out there and she's getting away!" I continue ranting. "I am your captain, and I'm telling you where to sail!"

Izzy spins around and begins to shout orders at the rest of the crew, falling in line.

Meanwhile, my eyes stay transfixed on the place where I'd seen Moby Butt just moments earlier, trying desperately to fight off the idea that maybe this whole thing had just been some wild flight of fantasy, a delusion brought on by my lack of sleep and the wee hours of the morning.

I shake my head vigorously, as though this movement could wash my mind clean of any doubt. I know what I saw out there.

The ship gradually begins to turn and then takes off in its new directly, the crew now standing sharp and ready as I continue to stare out at the water.

"Eyes peeled, ladies!" I cry. "She could swim off on another course at any second!"

I leave out the fact that nobody else even *saw* Moby Butt the first time, let alone has eyes on a change in her direction.

We cruise along like this for an hour or so, during which time I can sense the crew growing more and more weary. They don't let on for a second, but I can feel it in the air, sense the frustrated gloom that hangs above this great ship like some black raincloud, chasing us while we embark on this never ending pursuit.

I can tell the crew is afraid to give up, terrified of what might happen when someone dares suggest we slow down a bit or resume our previous course. They're right to be worried, but eventually even *I* begin to realize this particular jaunt will likely be fruitless.

Izzy steps up behind me, "Ma'am, would you like the crew to stay up on deck much longer?" my first mate questions. "There's a lot to do around the ship this morning and I think a few of them would like to get started."

I take a deep breath and let it out, then nod. "Yes, fine."

Izzy turns around and starts barking orders at the crew of women, sending them scattering as we slow down to our usual speed. When she's finished switching gears, she turns back towards me, walking over and standing next to the rail as we gaze out across the water together.

"We'll get Moby Butt next time," I say.

There's a long silence as the tension builds between us. If it were any other crewmember I would've already punished them severely for simply giving off a vague air of doubt, but Izzy and me have known each other for a very long time. She's not entirely safe from my wrath, but she can get away with much more than the others.

"The girls are talking," Izzy informs me. "They think a visit back home to the port would be good for morale. We've been headed out for so long that I'm starting to worry about ever getting back."

"We've got enough food," I state flatly.

"Not at this rate," Izzy counters. "In fact, if we *do* turn around now we'll still have to spend three nights without a proper supper."

I scoff. "Propper supper. This is a boat, not a luxury hotel."

"I know, but these conditions are more than just uncomfortable, Captain Amber. They're making it difficult to work. Response times are down. Mistakes are being made. We just need a few nights on land again to get our heads straight."

"And what of I?" I demand to know, finally turning to face my first mate. "Will I have my head on straight knowing that Moby Butt is still out here, swimming around with that beautiful round rump of hers? Teasing me in a playful erotic way?"

"I suppose not, Ma'am," Izzy replies.

"No!" I shout. "We will not turn around until the butt has been caught!"

Izzy hesitates for a moment, taking in a long breath and then letting it out slowly. I can tell she doesn't want to say the words that are sitting at the edge of his lips, but is forced into it for reasons I'm simply unwilling to hear out.

"What if you never catch the great round butt?" Izzy questions.

I'd had a suspicion this question was coming, and emotionally I've been able to prepare. Still, no amount of forethought could quell the powerful rage that suddenly floods through my bloodstream. Of course, I've questioned our journey this way before, but never said the words out loud.

Besides, this is *my* mission to question, *my* erotic ride that I've graciously paid the crew to come along for.

For a brief moment I actually consider throwing Izzy overboard, not to hurt her, but to give her a good fright before circling back and picking her up again.

Somehow, I manage to hold myself back, seething as I tightly grip the rail before me. My thoughts are a storm of lighting and thunder that rages with so much violence even *I'm* not sure what will become of it.

I suddenly hear a cracking sound as the bannister I'm holding onto splinters, the wood splitting as a few piece tumble down into the ocean below.

"I'm sorry," Izzy immediately blurts, trying to course correct. "I didn't mean it, Captain Amber."

"I think it's best you return to your quarters for a while," is all that I can think to say, the words hissing out through clenched teeth.

Izzy nods and hurries away, leaving me to stand and stare like every day before this.

In this particular moment, however, I'm determined to put an end to the cycle of torment. Despite the reaction it elicited from me, there remains a good point in Izzy's comments. We can't just keep going on and on like this, but we also can't turn around. Therefore, the next time I encounter Moby Butt, I will not turn back, and I will not give up. I will catch my lover and give her the kiss that has gone some seven years in the making, a playful game of cat and mouse that has evolved beyond even my wildest dreams.

It's all or nothing.

After 4 days of circling the area, there has still been no sign of Moby Butt.

I the mean time, the crew has grown nothing but more and more restless, still not daring the speak of their disappointment in words, but showing it through the eyes as they gaze constantly downward at the deck under their feat. They are frustrated and defeated.

To make matters worse, a storm has rolled in, darkening the skies above and pelting us with torrential rain. The waves are large and looming, just barely safe enough to navigate onward, and even still, some seasoned sailors would likely recommend against it.

It's in the early evening when I see it, that familiar double hump of Moby Butt's glorious buns as they peek out from the waves.

My heart nearly stops when I spot her, a validation of my insistence that this is where they sentient butt would be swimming.

"Thar she blows!" I scream, pointing out through the crashing waves.

The rest of the crew glances over, likely expecting to see nothing at all and then shocked to find I'm right. There, in plain view of the entire ship, is Moby Butt.

Immediately, we turn to the port side, now riding awkwardly against the waves as they crash down upon our wooden vessel. In any other situation this maneuver would be desperately avoided, but right now the crew knows there are worse things to come from us not catching up with these glorious sentient buns.

I quickly run to the front of the ship, where a cannon with a spring-loaded net has been mounted. The rules of our erotic game are simple, if I catch Moby Butt in the net, then she's officially been captured and our little journey ends. We'll likely kiss for a bit, then immediately head back to the shore for two glasses of ice cold chocolate milk on the beach.

This is the closest the giant rump has gotten to our ship in quite some time, and as my finger rests on the trigger of this locked and loaded net canon it takes every bit of discipline I can muster to hold myself back. I only have one shot here, and it has to be just right.

"Hey!" calls out Moby Butt from the churning gray water in a beautiful singsong tone. "Still looking for me?"

"Get back here you damn butt!" I cry, the rain hammering against my face as our vessel pushes forward through the whipping wind and crashing ocean waves.

"Gotta catch me first, cutie!" the sentient rump giggles, swimming quickly away from the boat.

This time we're ready for her, managing to keep a pace with the beautiful butt despite her most valiant attempts to pull away.

Suddenly, Izzy runs up behind me, crying out against the loud cacophony of the storm. "Ma'am!" she yells. "We can't head in this direction much longer! The waves are crashing down on the deck too hard. It's gonna break the mast clean in half."

"Then so be it!" I scream. "I'll have Moby Butt in my net and we'll drift to shore together!"

"Captain Amber, we'll sink if we keep going like this!" Izzy continues. "It's not just the mast! If the mast breaks we'll be stuck in this position for the rest of the storm. We'll start taking on water and we'll go under!"

I do my best to block out the ramblings of my first mate, who continues to scream into my ear while I line up the net canon with this giant swimming butt before me.

I realize suddenly Moby Butt is in range, and in this moment the entire world seems to shut down around me. Everything goes silent as reality comes to a standstill.

I pull the cannon's trigger.

There's a loud crack as my net erupts outward, but in this exact moment an extra large wave comes cascading down and slows against our ship, turning us to the side and sending my net off at a slightly canted angle.

I watch with wide eyes as it sails through the air and lands in the raging water before me, just barely catching one of Moby Butt's large rumps, but only serving to slow her down a bit. Unfortunately, the wave has also cracked the mast, and although we're not completely dead in the water, we've also been reduced to a crawl.

"No!" I scream, belligerent with anger. My big moment was a complete failure, but there's no turning back now.

Without thinking, I run to the edge of the boat and leap off into the icy ocean below. "I'll get you Moby Butt!" I scream.

I land in the water with a great splash, suddenly overwhelmed by the churning sensation of these powerful waves. I'm swimming against them as hard as I can but the force is just too strong, pulling me deep down into the sea and causing my body to twist and tumble the entire way. I no longer know which was is up or down, but through it all I can still catch slight glimpses of the gorgeous rump as she swims away from me.

"Still can't catch me!" Moby Butt calls out teasingly, her voice faint and strange in the dark, swirling water.

I refuse to give up, my arms aching and tired as I continue to struggle against the current. Despite my best efforts I can feel myself sinking deeper and deeper into the depths, losing strength as the life drains for my body.

Still, I will not let Moby Butt get the best of me.

"Bye bye!" the giant sentient butt calls.

I no longer have any idea where she is, the salty water now completely black all around me. My lungs feel as though they're about to explode, desperate for a breath of air.

Finally, at long last, I realize it might be a good idea to pump the breaks. This has gotten a little out of hand.

With my last gasp I call out into the water with our safe word, which is actually a complete sentence, desperately hoping Moby Butt will hear me. "Towards your butt I trot, you beautiful rump, to the last caress with thee: from heck's heart I kiss at thee, for love's sake I call my last breath at thee!"

With this, everything fades away.

The first thing I hear before I open my eyes is the wind, not a powerful raging storm, but a soft and gentle breeze through the swaying trees. I can hear water against the shore, but it does not crash, just pulses with a soft hiss.

I open my eyes to find I'm lying half submerged in the gentle waves of a desolate, sun soaked beach. There are palm trees lining the cove, and not a single sign of life other than the enormous humps of Moby Butt that rest some twenty yards out into the water.

"What happened?" I blurt, sitting upright. "Where's the ship."

Moby Butt laughs. "That's sweet. I love that you're worried about your crew after all that."

"Well?" I question, desperate for answers.

"They're fine, baby. They're fine," the sentient rump informs me. "The mast was cracked, but I was able to tow them back to shore for some much needed rest."

I let out a long sigh of relief, suddenly gravely embarrassed that I let it all get this far.

"I'm sorry," I finally offer.

Moby Butt laughs. "It's fine, but... yeah... that got a little out of hand."

I shake my head, astonished by my own actions.

"But there's a good lesson in there," the giant butt offers.

"What's that?" I question.

"Don't be afraid to use your safe word," Moby Butt continues. "That's what it's there for! I understand it can be a little embarrassing to call off the fantasy, but it's *very* important to communicate with your partner. You followed me for seven years!"

"You're right," I reply with a sigh.

We sit in silence for a moment, basking in the tropical sun.

"Where are we?" I finally question.

"Just some island out in the middle of nowhere," replies the living butt with a coy smile. "I thought you could use a little vacation yourself."

"Definitely," I offer with a nod.

The living butt smiles. "You know… there's nobody else around for miles."

I know exactly what she's getting at, and despite my intense physical exhaustion, I'm happy to play along. This time, however, there's no running away.

I climb to my feet and begin to wade out into the crystal clear water, farther and farther until, eventually, I dive in completely. I'm swimming now, approaching the glorious humps of my lover.

The second Moby Butt and I meet our hands are all over each other. I begin to kiss her passionately as she strips away my clothing, pulling the fabric from my body and letting it sink to the sand below. Soon enough, I'm completely naked, aching to be touched by this beautiful woman that I've so desperately yearned for.

"Let me get you off," the giant ass coos.

The next thing I know, Moby Butt is reaching down with one hand and gently rubbing my clit in soft, slow circles. I let out a slight whimper as she works me, getting me off with an incredible amount of grace and patience.

I float next to the sentient butt like this for a good while, my eyes closed as I enjoy this moment of utter peace. I feel absolutely content in a way that I haven't felt in ages, completely at ease in the arms of my lover.

I pump my hips against Moby Butt as her movements gradually quicken, rubbing me with more and more enthusiasm. In the pit of my stomach I can feel the first glorious hints of orgasm starting to blossom, the sensation bubbling up inside me and then pouring down my arms and legs. The next thing I know, my entire frame is overwhelmed with a strange, erotic hum, my body vibrating in a way that's difficult to describe.

I realize suddenly I haven't so much as orgasmed once during those seven years. I'm desperate to explode, aching to finally get the release I've been waiting for.

"Oh fuck, just like that! Just like that!" I start to groan, repeating the words over and over again as my eyes roll back into my head.

It's not long before the tension within me is simply too much to contain. The next thing I know, I'm erupting in a powerful fit of orgasm, completely losing myself in the moment as my body is flooded with sensation. I grip tight onto the enormous floating butt in the water before me, enjoying her warmth against my skin as we share this moment. I feel as though time is stretching out in an infinite wash of sensations, my physical form blending with my true spiritual self, free from the desperation of the chase that has haunted me so oppressively.

So what if I used my safe word? That's nothing to be ashamed of in any way, shape or form. That's trust and communication, and trust and communication is what love's all about.

Moby Butt keeps rubbing me at a steady pace until all the sensations have finished sweeping through me. When I finally finish I fall back into the water, but we're not done yet.

"Now it's your turn," I coo playfully.

I dive down into the salty sea, kicking my feet as I swim beneath the sentient rump's giant curve. It's not long before Moby Butt's beautiful pussy comes into view, and I immediately head towards it. When I reach her clit, I begin to rub it gently, pacing myself but also remembering that my air supply is limited.

Moby Butt begins to move along with the pace of my hand, clearly enjoying herself, but soon enough I'm forced to come back up for air, erupting through the surface and taking in an enormous gasp.

"What are you doing?" Moby Butt cries out. "Don't stop!"

I center myself and dive back in once again, hurrying to my lover's aching pussy and immediately getting back to work. This time, however, I change over from my hand to my tongue, lapping away at her pussy with erotic confidence. Moby Butt begins to shake, only this time her vibrations are much harder than before. I can tell the pleasure within her is escalating, building up well past its previous limits and threatening to erupt.

Fortunately, before my lungs start to hurt, I can feel the living butt clench tight and release in a powerful orgasm. Moby Butt screams loudly, her voice echoing across the cove as the blissed out sensations pulse across the entirety of her massive sentient ass.

When my beautiful lover finally finishes I swim to the surface, breaking through and then swimming over to hold her in my arms.

"The chase was fun, but so is this," I gush.

Moby Butt smiles. "Maybe we'll try it again someday, but for now, there's no place that I'd rather be than here in your arms."

.

EATEN RIGHT BY THE MYSTERIOUS SYMBOL EVERYONE USED TO DRAW

You never really know the path that lies ahead of you in life. You can try your best to predict it, to analyze every angle and come up with a plan for the future, but there are just too many branches on this tree to account for them all. Really, it's just a great big mystery, and it's a mystery you'll never get to the bottom of until it's right there in front of you, when the future becomes the present.

One day we might be sitting with our friend at work, sketching out a few ideas for a new graphic design assignment, and the next thing you know a mystery symbol is catching your, drawing you into an international hunt that will consume your entire life.

"What's that?" I question, pointing to a small sketch on the edge of my friend's notebook page.

Alice laughs. "You don't remember that? It's just the logo for that clothing brand from the 90s."

I narrow my eyes, not quite buying this explanation.

The symbol is innocent enough, a simple rendering of the letter S made from two rows of three vertical lines a piece. A couple more diagonal lies connect them in such a way that the letter appears in as strange, diamond-like shape. Its unique but also strangely familiar, something that I've seen a thousand times but can't quite to put my finger on where or when.

"Are you sure?" I question.

"Pretty sure," Alice says, stopping her work. "It's the Stummy S, from the Stummy clothing brand."

We're under a tight deadline at the moment, and this is far from what I should be concerned with right now, but I still can't help but follow my curiosity down the rabbit hole. I slide over and grab my laptop computer, opening it up and doing a quick image search for the 'Stummy S'.

I handful of results appear, but none of them resemble anything close to the image on Alice's notebook.

"Nope," I inform her. "That's not where it's from."

My friend scoots up next to me and gazes over my shoulder, taking in the search results and then finally admitting she was mistaken.

"That's... super weird," is all she can think to say.

"If it's not from a clothing brand then why is it so familiar?" I question, more to myself than anyone else.

"I can't really remember the first time I drew it," Alice admits. "It's like I always knew what it was, but that's not possible, obviously. I must've learned it from some other kid at school or something."

"Me too," I offer, "but where did *they* learn it?"

This question hangs in the air between us for a long while until, finally, I break the tension with a long sigh and a shrug. "Well... whatever."

Alice and me return to the notebook and start working out some new ideas for the task at hand, diving back in as the clock ticks down. We need to get five solid ideas back to the team upstairs by five, and right now I'm not exactly happy with any of them.

For a few minutes my friend and I are extremely focused, but as the time rolls on I find myself losing focus once more. At first, my mind just begins to wander aimlessly, but soon enough I realize where things are headed. I'm searching my memory banks, still trying to figure out the origin of that bizarre S symbol.

"Mary... Mary..." Alice repeats in my ear.

Suddenly, the sound of my own name breaks me out of this trancelike daze. I glance over at Alice, who's wearing a concerned look on her face.

"What's up?" my friend questions.

"I'm still thinking about that stupid symbol," I finally admit.

"Oh god," Alice blurts, more than a little frustrated at this point. "Are you going to be able to finish this assignment with me?"

I shake my head, admitting defeat. "I don't know. My mind's just not in this zone right now."

"It's fine," Alice replies, surprisingly understanding given the circumstances. "I'll cover for you, but just this once. Head home early if you need to."

"Really?" I question.

My friend nods. "But you've gotta get behind whatever designs I come up with while you're not here, okay? If you go home then you can't turn this around on me later."

"I promise," I reply. "Thank you."

I hug my friend and quickly gather my things, my mind racing with possibility. I'll readily admit my obsession with this unusual symbol is startlingly over-the-top, but my awareness of this fact doesn't make it any easier for me to stop myself.

Suddenly, a bolt of fear shoots through my body. What if there is no finite answer to this question, yet my desire to know even more just never relents? What if I can't even perform my job as my attention is pulled towards some unsolvable mystery?

I need to get to the bottom of this, and fast.

Soon enough I'm heading towards the elevator, taking it down to the lobby and making my way out of the office. Instead of heading towards the parking lot, however, I change course entirely.

I'd certainly be able to focus at home, but I'm looking for a place to dive deep into my research. The public library is only a block or so from here, and they'll have everything I need to find the source of this mysterious S.

As I walk down the street I find my pace growing more and more brisk, anxious to see what I can find. From deep within the subconscious parts of my mind ideas are bubbling forth, theories about how this strange symbol could've manifested into reality. Alice grew up in Sydney, Australia, and I'm from here in New York, meaning the power of this S isn't beholden to borders.

Soon, my thoughts are traveling a mile a minute, flashing through my head in rapid succession before shooting off in a variety of different directions.

When I reach the front steps of the library I've practically broken out into a jog, running up to the door and throwing it open as I make my way inside. I head directly to the front desk.

"Hello there," says the woman behind the counter. "How can I help you?"

"Where's the section on symbols?" I question.

The librarian smiles and nods. "Aisle two hundred and six, row seventy five to eight hundred and nine," she offers. "Is there any particular type of symbol you're looking for?"

"Alphabets? Letters?" I reply, not entirely sure how to put this into words.

"Row Seventy nine," the woman continues to clarify.

I thank her and then begin my trek across the library, still trembling with excitement. The more I walk, the more astonished I am by the size of the place, and grow even more amazed when I discover the section for symbol research is absolutely enormous.

I stand before a giant bookshelf that towers to the ceiling, gazing up at it like it's some buried archeological wonder. With no idea where to even begin, I start at the top, opening up the first book on the shelf and scanning through it to see what I can find.

For the next few hours I just read, my eyes scanning across page after page of material as I dig deeper and deeper into this strange new world. I'm on a hunt, but I'm not exactly sure what I'm looking for. It becomes apparent very quickly that none of these books will have a direct answer about the mysterious S, but that doesn't mean a clue doesn't lie somewhere within this seemingly endless stack of pages.

The sun has long gone down when I finally discover my first reference to the S. I'm flipping through some selected photographs when I see something faintly in the background of an image that makes me stop in my tracks. This particular book dates all the way back to the medieval times, and shows a variety of different ideas for illustrating the borders of ancient manuscripts. One of these methods looks exactly like that mysterious S.

"Oh my god," I stammer, unable to tear my eyes away from the page before me.

I'd assumed the creation of this symbol had occurred some time in the recent past, but *this* information was first published over five hundred years ago.

Reading the sidebar, I quickly learn that this border was made popular through writing and illustration at the Brimbo Castle, which still remains as a set of ruins in the English countryside.

I don't even think twice, pulling out my phone and searching for tickets on the next flight overseas.

The journey to Brimbo Castle has been long, grueling and expensive, but every time I consider pulling back on the throttle of this adventure I find myself immediately swayed by the powerful temptation of learning more. There's a mystery box just waiting for me to open it, a final answer to this riddle that I now realize has been tempting people since the long, long ago in the ancient world.

I pull up my rental car and park before the castle ruins.

At this point in history, people are free to walk these grounds whenever they'd like, the historical site now completely open to the public. It seems to have fallen out of favor, however, as there's nobody else here and it doesn't appear that visitors have made the trek in quite a while.

I climb out and begin strolling up towards the stone building, taking note of the way it has collapsed over time in various places. There's no longer a roof or floors, just a completely open structure where green grass has blossomed up and taken over. It's truly a beautiful sight.

I walk through the castle, not exactly sure what I'm looking for but paying close attention to every detail I can find. The building layout is quite difficult to get a full understanding of, planned with little rhyme or reason and especially confusing now that the original walls have partially collapsed.

"Why would the entryway be over here?" I say aloud to myself, narrowing my eyes as I gaze across these bizarre ruins.

In an effort to make sure I can see the whole building and leave no stone unturned, I begin to make a map of the structure, sketching out the walls as I walk along them. I don't make it very far before stopping suddenly, gasping at the symbol I've sketched out on the paper in my hand. This entire castle was constructed in the shape of my mysterious S, and above it is a separate section built to create an arrow pointing off into the nearby woods.

My heart is slamming hard within my chest now as I head off across the field in the direction of this arrow.

The thick green forest looms before me, and suddenly I get a sharp twinge of panic deep within. The sun has just started to make its decent, and I'm not entirely sure how deep into the woods I'll need to go.

Hell, I'm not even sure what I'm looking for is still there. These ruins are ancient, and the answer to this puzzle could've been stolen away many years before I was even born.

Still, I've gotta try.

Soon enough, I'm surrounded by trees, cutting my own path up into the hillside through the overgrowth. If there was ever a time when a trail existed here, that time has long since passed.

I walk for what seems like forever, the sun gradually drifting lower and lower in the sky until the colors above begin to change and transform, shifting from light blues to a deep purple and brilliant orange. Even if I turn back now, I won't be back to my car before nightfall.

Suddenly, I stop in my tracks, gazing up at an enormous cliffside before me. Of course, the cliffside isn't all that draws my attention, it's the familiar symbol carved into its base. There, carved deep into the rock and covered in moss is the mysterious, universal S symbol. Below it lies an open, gaping maw of a cave.

My breathing heaving and my heart pounding hard within my chest, I make my way up to the cave entrance. I peer deep into the darkness, knowing full well that the only option is to continue onward, but still incredibly frightened by the prospect.

With no other options let, I cautiously begin to make my way into the shadows of this rocky opening, diving deeper and deeper into the cold, wet hole. Stalactites hang down from above, and on them dangle a handful of large bats who pay me no mind.

Fortunately, before the cave gets too dark and cold, it actually starts to lighten up again. I begin to see torchlight, and soon enough I find that the walls on either side of me are lined with several rows of flame, lighting the path onward. Along the cool hard ground several beautiful rugs have been laid out, as though someone has been waiting for me to arrive.

I follow the path, twisting and turning deeper into the mountainside until arriving at a wooden door built directly into the rock. More light cascades out from under it.

Not knowing what else to do, I step up and knock.

"Uh... hello?" I call out. "Is anyone in there?"

"Come in," replies a voice, sweet and soft. "Come in and find what you've sought for so long!"

I open the door slowly and peer within to find a well-furnished room lit by several burning torches. There before me, standing in the middle of the chamber with a wide smile on her face, is the sentient embodiment of this mysterious S.

"Oh my god," I blurt. "It's you!"

The S floats towards me with a smile, then reaches out and extends her hand, which I shake.

"Hello, I'm the letter S," she says, "but you can call me Sasha."

"I'm Mary," I inform her.

When I pull my hand away I notice a small slip of paper within my palm. Trembling, I open it up and read aloud the message written within.

"This coupon entitles you to one free dictionary. Conditions apply," I recite.

I narrow my eyes, utterly confused.

"That's... not actually valid anymore," Sasha informs me. "I still have to hand them out, though. I'm sorry but you're a little late on finding me."

"What do you mean? What is this?" I stammer.

"Viral marketing for the alphabet," the living S states bluntly.

"Wait, what?" I blurt.

Sasha nods. "I've been here for thousands of years. When the alphabet first started, they were trying to figure out some cool ways to get people excited about it. I guess the suits decided that the letter S was a good place to kick things off, so they created this A. R. G."

"A. R. G?" I question.

"Alternate reality game," Sasha explains. "You know, people would remember this cool S they used to draw, then hunt down the clues and, eventually, find me. I used to give out coupons for stone tools and stuff like that, but then those fell off a bit. Now I give out dictionary coupons but, honestly, I think that's a little dated, too. They're all expired."

"Well, why are you still promoting the alphabet?" I ask, deeply troubled. "Everyone uses it already."

"They do?" Sasha questions.

I nod. "Yeah."

The sentient S considers this for a moment. "I guess it's been a while since anyone has come to see me. I didn't realize things had caught on so much."

Suddenly, the reality of this situation hits me like a truck, literally causing me to stagger back as I struggle to regain my footing. After all this searching, I've finally come to find that the *real answer* is I'm nothing more than a pawn in some viral marketing scheme from thousands of years ago.

I fall into a nearby chair, still trying to collect myself as I stare off into space.

"I'm sorry if you're disappointed," Sasha offers.

I shake my head. "It's fine. This is just not what I was expecting."

The living S continues to hover before me, and as I watch her I begin to find myself deeply empathizing with her position. I only had to take the weekend off from work, but Sasha has been here for thousands of years, and for what?

"Do you like hiding here in a cave?" I question. "Just waiting around for someone to solve the mystery?"

The floating S shrugs. "I guess. I mean... I don't know. There's a lot of stuff I've been curious about."

"What stuff?" I ask.

"What's it like to fly in a plane?" Sasha questions. "I see them in the sky sometimes when I walk to the edge of the cave."

"It's pretty cool," I admit. "You can get anywhere in the world in a matter of hours. It's not super comfortable, but it's very convenient compared to the alternative.

"Wow," is all that the living letter can say, her eyes alight with curiosity.

"Anything else?" I ask.

Sasha thinks about this for a moment. Eventually, her body language begins to change, softening a bit.

"What's it like to have sex?" she finally asks me.

"It depends on the person you're having sex with." I offer.

"With you." Sasha questions bluntly.

I consider her words for a minute, then finally take the leap. "Why don't you come over here and find out."

Suddenly, the building tension between us breaks as Sasha floats towards me. I spring up from my chair and meet her with a barrage of kisses, my hands making their way frantically across her beautiful body. Soon enough, the living S is stripping away my clothes, revealing my nude form to the cool cave air as a pleasant, erotic chill runs the length of my spine.

"This is so crazy," I murmur between kisses. "I've never been with a letter of the alphabet before, let alone a letter involved with a several thousand year viral marketing campaign."

"There's a first time for everything," Sasha offers.

Suddenly, the living letter is pushing me back again, causing me to collapse into my chair. She continues kissing me, but as she does this she brings her attention lower and lower across my feminine form. When she reaches my nipples she sucks on them a bit, teasing my breasts before continuing onward.

Eventually, the beautiful living symbol reaches my waist, where she hesitates slightly.

"Do you want me?" Sasha coos.

"Yes," I beg, quaking with anticipation.

"Beg for it," the sentient S continues.

"Please," I groan. "Please."

Finally, Sasha has mercy, slipping a single finger across my aching clit and getting to work as she begins to gently rub in soft circles. The second she touches me I can feel my entire form flooded with pleasant sensation, completely lost in the wave of bliss that now floods across my frame.

"Oh my god," I groan, closing my eyes tight and letting myself melt away into the chair. I'm utterly relaxed, thankful to be along on this erotic journey.

Soon enough, Sasha takes things to the next level by replacing her finger with the tip of her tongue. The beautiful letter crouches down before me and begins to lap away at my pussy, starting slowly at first and then gradually gaining speed.

Deep within the pit of my stomach I can feel the first hints of orgasm starting to brew, bubbling up from somewhere deep inside me and spilling out across my arms and legs. I can feel the tension building within, the impending climax looming higher and higher above with no sign of breaking.

Clearly, Sasha is good at what she does.

Putting this into practice, the sentient letter slides her fingers inside me, now working my body from two distinct sources. The sensation is absolutely incredible, and it only serves to make me ache for climax even more. I'm gripping the arms of the chair tightly, every muscle within my body pulled taut until finally the pressure is just too much to take and, suddenly, I'm erupting in a powerful fit of orgasm.

I throw my head back and let out a mighty scream, completely swept away by the blissed out sensations. I feel as though I've left my physical form, the pleasure just too much to maintain within my physical shell and forcing me to ascend to some strange astral plane above.

When the orgasm finally passes I collapse back in exhaustion, but instead of remaining tired and fucked silly, I find myself even more energized than before.

"Now it's your turn," I coo, pushing back against the living S.

I crawl down off the chair, taking Sasha with me as I push her back against the floor. I make my way down her beautifully drawn form, still marveling at just how perfect this design really is. When I reach her pussy I take my time, gently licking Sasha's clit while she begins to rock her hips against me. The movement of this beautiful sentient symbol is easy to fall into, and soon enough I begin to pace myself in time with her heaves.

All the while, I'm growing more and more firm with the strength of my tongue, pushing harder against her most sensitive areas. By the time I'm fully licking across her clit, Sasha has placed her hands against my head and is pulling me against her, taking control of the situation.

"Oh my fucking god, oh my fucking god," the sentient letter begins to moan, repeating the words over and over again. She's quiet at first, mumbling the phrase under her breath as she goes, but over time her cries grow louder and louder. Eventually, the beautiful S is screaming out at the top of her lungs, filling the cave with her erotic mantra. "Oh my fucking god! Oh my fucking god!"

I can sense the letter trembling hard, aching for release, and this only makes me stay the course even more. My oral skills have gotten me this far, there's no reason to change anything now.

Soon enough, Sasha's words begin to transform into something strange and unusual, a frantic squeal unlike anything I've ever heard. She's hovering right on the edge of climax, torn between worlds as her body struggles to keep up with the myriad of sensations.

Finally, when she's good and ready, I slip my fingers deep within her pussy, filling her up and sending this beautiful living letter hurtling over the edge. Sasha arches her back up as her body explodes with orgasmic sensation, quaking hard as she hisses through clenched teeth. She's completely lost in the moment.

When the beautiful letter finally finishes she collapses back against the rug below, panting with exhaustion. I crawl down next to her and cuddle up close, enjoying her warmth against my skin as the two of us bask in the sexual afterglow.

"Thank you for letting me share that with you," Sasha gushes.

I scoff. "Thank *you*. That was incredible."

"I'm sorry I'm just a viral marketing campaign," the sentient letter offers. "I know it was probably very hard for you to find this place. It must be kind of shitty to get here and realize the mystery isn't all that exciting after all."

I let out a long sigh, shaking my head. "I discovered something much more important than the answer to some silly riddle. I discovered you."

The two of us kiss deeply, enjoying the presence and warmth of one another in this otherwise dank, dark cave.

"Are you going to stay?" Sasha questions.

I nod. "It's a little dark to go walking back through the woods right now. Is that okay?"

"It's more than okay," she offers. "You can stay as long as you'd like."

"Actually," I reply. "I was thinking *you* might want to come back with *me*. I work at a design firm and I'm sure they'd love to have a living letter on staff."

"Really?" the sentient symbol questions, her eyes overflowing with excitement.

I nod. "And we'll knock another one off your buck list with a plane right home."

"This is perfect," the mysterious S says, no longer much of a mystery, but just as exciting.

LIGHTLY FLAVORED ZERO CALORIE CARBONATED WATER GETS ME OFF

Although it's been a long time since my last doctor visit, I can't ever remember it taking this long. Sitting here in my hospital gown, gazing at a chart of the human body that's been hung on the wall nearby, I actually start to worry something terrible has been discovered. This was supposed to be nothing more than a routine physical, a quick examination and then a flu shot to hold me over during the end of fall. At least, that's what I thought.

Now, I've got no clue what's going on. The nurses did some tests and seemed alarmed by my results, then decided to do a few more, and then another one, and another. All this happened before the doctor even had a chance to seem me, and now more than an hour has passed. I've still heard nothing.

I go through waves of anxiety just thinking about what could be happening out there, then reassure myself that, whatever it is, I've done my part to stay healthy. I eat right and exercise five days a week, keep an active social life and am generally pretty happy. What more do they want from me?

Suddenly, there's a sharp double knock on the office door. Before I have a chance to say anything, my doctor steps inside and nods towards me. She's holding a folder in her hand, gripping it tightly, along with a small black container.

"Johanna, how are you feeling today?" my doctor questions.

"Pretty good Dr. Scott," I reply. "At least, I *was* feeling pretty good."

"Oh yeah?" she raises her eyebrows.

"Then I got here and now I'm scared as hell," I admit.

Dr. Scott makes a strange, tightlipped expression, an awkward half smile that seems to only serve the purpose of hiding her true emotions.

"Is something wrong?" I continue.

Dr. Scott lets out a long sigh and opens up the folder, pulling out several charts and graphs. She begins to put them up on a rail built into the wall next to her, displaying the papers so I can see. "Well, there's a lot of good to talk about. Your general health is not too shabby. In fact, it's excellent. It's your blood that I'm worried about."

"My blood?" I stammer, not exactly sure what this means.

Dr. Scott nods. "I want to show you something."

My doctor pulls a small glass vial out of the black container she's been holding. She holds it up to the light so that I can get a good view.

"What does that look like to you?" the doctor questions.

I stare at the vial for a long while, trying to make sense of what I'm seeing. The liquid within is dark brown and bubbling, fizzing slightly as it sloshes around in its glass tube.

"I'm not sure," I finally admit. "Was that inside my body?"

Dr. Scott nods. "I'm afraid so."

My doctor untwists the tube's small cap and, without a second thought, throws back a quick swig of the substance.

"Oh my god!" I blurt, gasping as I reel from this unexpected maneuver.

Dr. Scott swallows, then nods approvingly. "It's pretty good, you want some?" She holds the vial out towards me, still half full.

"Is it safe?" I question.

"Oh yes, perfectly," my doctor assures me.

I hesitate for a moment, then finally decide to take the leap. I trust my doctor, after all, and she seems to be doing just fine after consuming the mysterious substance. I reach out and take the vial in my hand, giving the liquid one last look before taking a long, satisfying gulp. I take down the rest of the vial, leaving it empty.

Immediately, I recognize the taste. "That's cola," I blurt. "It's still fizzy. This was *inside* me?"

Dr. Scott nods. "It's running through your veins. In fact, you've got no blood left. You're entirely filled with soda."

"How is that possible?" I stammer. "I should be dead."

"Well, it's certainly not healthy, but so far you're doing fine," Dr. Scott explains. "However, it's putting a huge strain on your heart. How much cola would you say you drink per day, Johanna?"

"Per day?" I repeat back, deep in thought. "Just a can with dinner, probably."

"Probably?" the doctor questions.

I think about this a little longer, starting at the beginning of my day and then walking through my activities step by step. "Well, I get up and have my morning drink, which is cola, too, now that I think about it. Then I take a shower and get ready. I have breakfast, which normally has a soda on the side… hmm…"

"Sounds like we're already up to *triple* your initial guess," Dr. Scott informs me.

Now my mind is racing with all the various times I reach for a soda can throughout the day. I'm talking to myself like a mad woman now, calculating all the times I imbibe this sugary beverage.

"Then you've got one on the way to work, and another on the way home," I list, counting on my fingers. "There's the pre dinner cola along with the dinner cola."

"Let me stop you right there," Dr. Scott finally interjects. "Is there any time that you're drinking water?"

I scoff. "What? Why the hell would I wanna do that? I can afford soda."

"It's not about what you can afford," Dr. Scott explains. "It's about the health of your body. A little bit of cola is fine, but having the stuff course through your veins like this is not natural. There's gonna be devastating consequences once the soda starts wearing down your heart valves."

I consider her words for a long while. "So how many more cans of soda can I have?" I finally question.

"Literally none," Dr. Scott replies bluntly. "Frankly, you shouldn't even be able to speak, think, or move right now, and I'm shocked you're not in an overwhelming amount of pain. You're basically a walking miracle."

"Not even diet cola?" I continue.

My doctor just stares at me blankly. "No. Fortunately, there are some great alternatives on the market right now. Have you heard of La Groix?"

I shake my head.

"It's a lightly flavored, zero calorie carbonated water that comes in a can. I'm not super excited about the carbonation for you, but in this case I think the similarity to soda is really gonna help you switch over," Dr. Scott explains.

"Oh, great," I reply, nodding confidently. "I think I can try that. Where can I get some?"

"Pretty much everywhere," she continue, "but you're going to need *a lot* of the stuff, and you're gonna need it fast.'

As I stand before the completely empty shelf, the first thing that hits me is confusion. Clearly this must be some kind of mistake. I'm surrounded by all kinds of beverages, yet this particular section of my local grocery store is utterly bare.

I step back a bit then stroll down the aisle, looking closely for any sight of La Groix. My doctor assured me they would carry the stuff almost anywhere, and I could've sworn I'd seen it here before.

Eventually, my hunt returns me to empty shelf once again, just as perplexed as ever.

Fortunately, at this very moment a store employee strolls by.

I call out, grabbing their attention. "Hey, is there a section for lightly flavored zero calorie carbonated water?" I question.

The employee stops. "You're looking at it," he informs me.

I glance back and forth between the man and these empty shelves. "This is your La Groix section?"

The employee nods. "Crazy, huh? We just can't seem to keep the stuff in stock. Everyone's trying to switch over."

I'm suddenly struck by a wave of dread, realizing that my health is on the line. Dr. Scott was very insistent that I needed to make a change or suffer some dire, life threatening consequences.

I find myself gazing past the employee at a wall of various sugary sodas behind him, tempted by these familiar containers and logos. Would it be so bad if I just grabbed a six-pack of cola instead? Just to hold me over?

I shake my head vigorously, hoping to wash away the toxic thoughts within. This is serious.

The employee notices this fearsome mental battle that I'm currently experiencing and tries his best to offer some support. "You know, we've got plenty of bottled water if that's something you're interested in?"

The very thought of this option makes me physically ill. It's too much, too soon. I don't know if my body can handle that kind of change right out the gate. This is a whole new lifestyle that I'm hoping to ease myself into, and it's going to take multiple steps to get there. Right now, La Groix is my only option.

"I can't," I stammer.

"There's a few other stores nearby that carry lightly flavored zero calorie carbonated water," explains the employee, "but you're gonna want to get there on the day their shipments come in. This stuff gets bought up almost immediately."

"When did *your* last shipment come in?" I question.

The employee checks his watch. "Oh, it's been about twenty minutes now."

"Twenty minutes!" I blurt.

The employee nods. "Told you it goes quick."

My heart is slamming hard within my chest now as my distress grows, suddenly realizing that getting my hands on a case of La Groix is going to be damn near impossible. With every beat I can feel my heart starting to flood with painful sensation, the cola that surges through my veins finally beginning to get the best of me.

The employee notices the pained expression on my face. "You know, if you really wanna get ahold of this stuff then you should talk to the delivery women directly. Maybe you can snag some La Groix before it even reaches the shelves."

My eyes light up as I hear this. "Really?" I question. "How?"

"Well, every time she makes a drop off she goes across the street for lunch at that little café on the corner," the employee explains in a hushed tone. "If you hurry you can probably catch her before she leaves. You might be able to buy some La Groix straight off the truck."

Immediately, I spring into action, thanking the man for his help as I rush back towards the exit. The next thing I know I'm sprinting across the parking lot towards the restaurant on the corner.

I only get about halfway there when the pain hits again. It comes in a sudden burst, ripping through my chest and causing me to stumble to my knees. I collapse under the strain, gripping at my heart as though this simple movement might keep everything in order on its own. I should've known this kind of action would be too much.

Closing my eyes tight, I try my best to calm down, to pull myself back into some kind of alignment. The pain within me is still throbbing hard, but it's not growing. Instead, the sensation just sits on my shoulders like a heavy weight, pushing me towards the concrete below.

I finally take all the inspiration I can muster and put it towards one single movement: standing up again. Unfortunately, this particular maneuver is a lost cause, and the next thing I know I'm toppling down even more disastrously than before. My entire body hits the pavement, hard.

I feel as though I'm floating down a cool, calm river, completely at ease. Something within me has changed, and I can already feel it, but the second this realization hits me is the second I also realize it is all just a dream.

My eyes fly open and there directly above is a strange, rounded shape, it's metallic glint blocking out the sun.

I start to cough, sputtering wildly as a rush of liquid comes blasting out of my lungs in a burst of misty air.

What I now recognize as a sentient can of lightly flavored zero calorie carbonated water pulls back in amazement. A crowd that has gathered around us begins to cheer happily, breathing a collective sigh of relief as I return from my walk in the shadow realm. Applause fills my ears.

Weak and weary, I sit up and glance around, noticing now that my fall had attracted quiet a crowd. Even more likely, it's my resuscitation that has garnered so much attention.

"You took a pretty bad spill there," the La Groix can offers. "Are you alright? Do you need to go to the hospital?"

"I just came from the hospital," I inform her.

This just makes the sentient beverage even more concerned. "You seemed really dehydrated."

"It's more than that, but… yeah," I admit.

"Once I gave you a little taste you started waking up," the can explains. "It wasn't much, so you should really think about pounding some water as soon as you can."

I nod. "Thank you so much. I'm Johanna."

"Loba Crills," the beverage offers in return. "Nice to meet you. Can I ask, where were you headed in such a hurry."

I take a deep breath and then let it out, hesitating slightly and then realizing I have no real reason to keep this information to myself, other than embarrassment.

"I was trying to find the La Groix delivery woman," I admit. "I'm guessing you know her?"

As Loba and I continue to chat like this the crowd around us begins to dissipate, clearing out as they continue on with their daily errands.

Loba scoffs. "Know her, I *am* her."

"Oh!" I blurt. "Do you have any cases left?"

The sentient lightly flavored zero calorie carbonated water winces as I say this, shaking her head. "I'm sorry, I just dropped off the last off my shipment. There won't be another batch until next week and I'm pretty sure the stuff I dropped off is already gone. I'm sorry."

I try my best to keep the feelings of grave disappointment from showing up on my expression, but despite my best efforts I'm unable to hide the powerful emotions that surge through me. I'm lucky to be alive right now, but I'm also well aware that I'll only get so many chances to pull myself together.

Loba notices. "Hey, listen," she offers, leaning forward a bit and tipping herself towards me. "At least have some more while I'm here. It'll get you on the right track, maybe hold you over for a while."

I graciously accept, opening my mouth wide while the sentient beverage pours herself into me. At first it's a little too much, the water spilling out across my face as I struggle to lap it up, but we quickly find a balance together. In order to find the correct angle I end up pulling Loba close, our bodies now pressed tightly together, at which point a spark of something powerful shoots through me.

Yes, I'm feeling a great sense of relief at this water-based nourishment, but I'm also feeling a breathtaking amount of attraction to this living beverage. Loba is objectively beautiful, but it's not just her incredible good looks that draw me in. This lightly flavored zero calorie carbonated water doesn't need to care about me, doesn't need to spend her afternoon making sure I'm alright, but she seems genuinely happy to be here.

If I could, I'd stay like this forever, but eventually Loba pulls back and returns to her upright position. "That's all I can offer for now," she informs me. "I can't get too empty."

"It's okay," I reply. "Thank you so much. Lime, right? I can barely taste it."

Loba nods. "That's kinda the point."

The two of us just sit in each other's presence for a moment longer, our minds racing. In this awkward silence, it suddenly dawns on me that the arousal I feel for Loba might not be a one-way street. There's something in her eyes that hints at more, much more.

"You gonna be alright?" Loba finally questions, breaking the silence.

I nod. "I think so."

"You know, you can always just drink water from the faucet if you're getting thirsty," she reminds me.

"I know, I know," I reply. "I should probably start doing that."

"Probably?" Loba questions skeptically.

I shrug.

The living beverage takes a deep breath and then lets it out, finally reaching out her hand and pulling me to my feet. "Come on," she says. "You're coming with me."

I'm not quite sure what the lightly flavored zero calorie carbonated water means but this, just staring at her in utter confusion.

"I don't want you to end up fainting again," Loba continues. "Let's get lunch so I can keep an eye on you."

I'm happy to accept. Hopefully there's something more to her invitation than just a vague concern for my wellbeing.

Soon enough, the two of us are strolling back over to the café, where it appears the La Croix is still halfway finished with her meal. We return to Loba's table and I sit down across from her, the waiter strolling over to address is.

"Hello ma'am," the waiter offers, nodding in my direction. "Is there anything I can get for you?"

"I'm not really hungry," I inform him, "but I could definitely use something to drink. What kind of sodas do you have?"

I suddenly notice the intensity of Loba's stare, catching myself.

"I mean... do you have any La Groix?" I question, altering course away from my bad habits.

The waiter shakes his head. "Just the one you're sitting across from. Would you like some tap water?"

I start to reply and then stop suddenly, unable to form the words. "I...

I… I think I'll need another minute."

The waiter accepts this and then strolls away, leave Loba and me to decompress.

"You can't just get a water?" the sentient beverage questions.

"It's… very different from soda," I remind her. "Honestly, I just need a little La Groix to ease into it."

"Well, I appreciate your dedication to the product," the lightly flavored zero calorie carbonated beverage replies, "but this is a matter of life and death."

"I know," I reply, unable to look her in the eye.

When I finally glance up at Loba again, she's wearing an unexpected smile. It's hard to read the look on her face, but if I had to choose a single word I'd say: mischievous.

"You know I'd give you more if I could," Loba coos, "but I can't drain myself that low."

"I know," I assure her.

"We could always fill me up at bit first, though," the living beverage continues."Do you know how La Groix is made?"

I shake my head.

"Well, it comes from larger, sentient cans like myself," Loba explains. "There are a few ways to fill us up, but the quickest way is through arousal."

I nearly fall over backwards in my chair when she says this. "Oh, really?" I stammer.

Loba nods. "Do you think you'd be interested in helping me out with that? It'd be a great deal for both of us."

The waiter suddenly returns. "Have you made any decisions?" he questions.

"I think we were just about to leave, actually," I inform him.

The second the living La Groix and I enter her apartment our clothes are coming off, stripping each other down as we give in to the potent arousal that courses through our bodies. Since we've left the restaurant the tension has only built and built, and now it's finally allowed to release in an explosion of passion.

Loba and I quickly get to work exploring one another's bodies, our hands enjoying this new topography as we tremble and quake with anticipation. The living beverage's attention draws lower and lower across my form until she reaches my waist, hesitating there and refusing to go any lower.

"Do you want it?" she questions. "Do you want that lightly flavored goodness?"

"Yes," I groan, my eyes shut tight as I press against the form of her can.

"Good," Loba replies, finally having mercy as she slides her finger down across my clit.

I let out a startled gasp as she touches me, knowing the sensation was coming but not entirely prepared for the reality of this situation. Loba definitely knows what she's doing, slowly rubbing back and forth across my most sensitive areas as the sensations within me build.

"Oh my god," I groan, the words slipping out from my mouth as I begin to pump my hips in time with Loba.

It's not long before me and my lightly flavored zero calorie carbonated water fall into a rhythm together, recognizing the best way that our bodies move and flow. Over time, the movement of Loba's hand speeds up, as does the sway of my hips.

I've never been able to cum standing up like this, but the more time that passes in this position, the more I feel like it's a goal that might actually be possible. When Loba makes her next move, however, I'm certain of it.

The next thing I know this sentient beverage is dropping down to her knees before me, gazing up with hungry eyes as she dives in and begins to lap away at my pussy. The gorgeous living object slips her fingers within me as she works, now filling my body with pleasure from two distinct sources. The sensation is incredible, the feelings within me swirling like a whirlpool of carnal, erotic passion.

"Oh fuck," I stammer, gripping tightly onto Loba's rounded metallic body. "I'm so close. I'm so fucking close."

I'm trembling much harder than before, but this time it's not just out of anticipation. There's a myriad of sensations within my body and they're all fighting for space, spilling into one another in new, exciting ways as the quickly run out of room.

"Just like that, just like that," I repeat over and over again, my eyes rolling back into my head as Loba continues to work me. "Just like that, just like that!"

The feelings build and build until, suddenly, I just can't take the pressure any longer. The next thing I know I'm erupting like a volcano of sensation, my whole body swept away in a powerful tidal wave of orgasm. I'm completely lost in the moment, my eyes rolling back into my head as every muscle within my body releases its tension at the same time.

I throw my head back as the repetitive phrase that so passionately spilled from my mouth transforms into a frantic howl, no words available to sum up the magic that's happening within.

When I finally finish I stumble back a bit, releasing my grip on the beautiful can. Loba seems to be very happy about the job well done, and even more happy that I'm thrilled to return the favor.

I take a brief moment to gather my senses then suddenly I'm moving back towards the lightly flavored zero calorie carbonated water, pushing her away so that she falls into the chair behind her. I continue forward, dropping down onto my hands and knees as I crawl towards Loba seductively. I sway my hips from side to side as I move, giving the living beverage a good look at my beautiful body.

"You like what you see?" I question.

Loba nods.

I push up even farther until I'm directly before the can's pussy, running my tongue along her in two playful licks.

"You like what you feel?" I continue.

Loba nods again.

"Good," I coo, then dive in completely, swirling my tongue gently around the carbonated water's aching clit.

Despite my enthusiasm, I take my time with Loba, getting to know the pulse of her body as I work her. I start off slowly and then allow the two of us to find a synchronization, moving together as one. With every passing second, the living beverage relaxes just a little bit more, until eventually she's fully open to the moment as it comes, accepting every bit of sensation that I'm willing to give her.

Deep within Loba's aluminum can frame I can here a strange noise beginning to crackle and pop, the carbonated water filling within.

She's getting close.

I let Loba enjoy herself for quite a while, keeping her balanced on the edge until finally I push her over and give her what appears the be the best orgasm of her life. The living beverage is completely out of control, screaming out at the top of her lungs as her body spasms and shakes.

When she finally finishes, Loba falls back into the couch cushions behind her, exhausted.

"That was incredible," I offer.

"It was," Loba replies with a smile. "I think I'm all filled up again. You want a sip?"

I nod. "Yeah, but let's save it for later."

I stand up and stroll over to the living beverage's kitchen, grabbing an empty glass from the cupboard and approaching the tap. I turn it on and fill up my glass, then take a massive swig of the water. Not so bad after all.

"Whoa," is all that Loba can think to say.

"I need to get used to this," I remind her. "You're so sweet and generous, but I don't wanna drain you too much."

"That's... really nice," the living beverage informs me with a twinkle in her eye, "but you can always just fill me up again."

"You mean...?" I start.

Loba nods, beckoning me back over to her with a wide smile on her rounded aluminum face.

ABOUT THE AUTHOR

Dr. Chuck Tingle is an erotic author and Tae Kwon Do grandmaster (almost black belt) from Billings, Montana. After receiving his PhD at DeVry University in holistic massage, Chuck found himself fascinated by all things sensual, leading to his creation of the "tingler", a story so blissfully erotic that it cannot be experienced without eliciting a sharp tingle down the spine. Chuck's hobbies include backpacking, checkers and sport.

Printed in Great Britain
by Amazon

46687811R00050